MW01125051

For Kerry, Katie, Bret and Tess

My consolation is that
everything that has been is eternal:
the sea will cast it up again.

Nietzsche, *The Will to Power*

Note to the Reader

This is a work of fiction. Although some of the characters in this story have analogues in the real world, these fictional versions are entirely imaginary. Their actions and their spoken words as described in this book never took place. Nor did the struggle to uncover a mole within the ranks of the CIA ever occur. And although the author of this book spent eight years as a stringer for *People* magazine (1988-1996), the imaginary version of *People* magazine portrayed in this book bears no resemblance to the *People* magazine of 1995 or any other year.

—Tom Nugent

SUNDAY

1. HURT BY MR. SINATRA

Frank Sinatra made a pistol of his right hand.

He aimed it at the stringer's nose.

"Who the hell are *you*?" he asked.

"Me? No problem! I'm a stringer, sir. For *People*. You know, the magazine?"

The famous blue eyes grew much larger. Frankie was obviously pissed. "How the hell did you get past Arnoldo and Rocky? Why are you in my dressing room?"

"Could I interview you, sir? I'll keep it short. Three minutes would be terrific. Two minutes, even. Heck, I could probably get what I need in 45 seconds! Here you are, 79 years old, at an age when most performers –"

"Not a chance," snapped Ol' Blue Eyes. "I'm about to do a *concert*, for shit's sake. My *last* public concert, probably. Besides, I don't talk to youse bums. Youse guys from the press? Bums! What are you, a magazine guy? You're garbage, you bum! All my life, I been fighting off youse bums. Total garbage, all of youse." The brand-name Adam's apple quivered, then jumped. "How the hell did you get past Rocky?"

But the stringer ignored this query. "Won't take but a sec, sir, 'cause I only have two basic questions. First: Why are your hundreds of hit songs so incredibly popular? And second: Why are you, yourself, so wonderful? Personally, I mean?"

Sinatra began to scream. They were the screams of a world-class baritone, so they came across loud and clear. "Hey! Hey! Arnoldo! Rocky! Who is this guy? Who *is* this guy? We got garbage in here—hop to it, you imbeciles!"

Two large gentlemen instantly materialized. The stringer noted the prominent bulges in their Armani suits. As with Mr. Sinatra, both Arnoldo and Rocky appeared to be of thoroughly Italian descent. Their lush hair was dark, oily, swept back in scalloped waves like ebony-hued ice cream. Their eyes were huge and golden-brown and full of an inconsolable Mediterranean grief. Utterly crestfallen, the two disgraced gunmen hung their great heads together while the world-famous American crooner chewed them out royally. "What's with you two morons, anyhow? I'm paying you fabulous sums, for shit's sake! Do something, dipshits! Who *is* this guy?"

Because they had no answer for him, the dipshits simply nodded in unison, then turned to confront the intruder. Once roused to action, they seemed surprisingly cheerful about the task that lay ahead. Grinning like jovial gangsters in some lighthearted musical, the bodyguards radiated both professional menace and a brisk, carefree *bonhomie*. Moving with surprising swiftness, they pressed their massive bodies against the much smaller body of the stringer. But they were careful not to touch him with their hands. Relying exclusively on their great bulk, they danced him toward a yellow door marked EXIT.

"Mr. Sinatra!" the stringer bleated helplessly as the door approached. "Won't you tell *People* why you're so wonderful? Puh-leeeeeease? Here you are, 79 years old, and yet you just released another hit album—*Duets II*—only last year! What a legend! What an inspiration for America's senior citizens! Still performing onstage, and you're nearly 80! Mr. Sinatra, we've got 26 million readers out there, and they'll be hanging on your every syllable!"

"Get lost, youse bozo."

"I see. So that's how it is? Well, I do thank you for making your wishes clear. Perhaps you'd prefer to talk at some other time? Tell you what... I'll phone your press agent first thing tomorrow morning. Would that work for you, Mr. S?"

But the man in the jet-black tuxedo had turned away. He was snorting now, woofing loudly: "Goddam magazine garbage... sneaks into my dressing room. Who is this guy?" And then a moment later, the smiling giants in the expensive tailoring had nudged the stringer through EXIT and the big steel doors had slammed shut behind him.

All at once, Tommy Moon was no longer inside the Baltimore Convention Center, where thousands of Sinatra fans had gathered for this Sunday Evening *Fight Lupus!* Benefit Concert. Now the stringer was *outside* the jam-packed concert venue. And it was raining out here, raining hard. He tried the heavy doors a couple of times, pushed at them helplessly, ineffectually. The doors were locked and steel-barred and utterly impregnable.

Too bad. Had all justice, all decency fled the planet? Why do men live, anyway? And while we're at it, why do *women* live? Do they live for the same reason that men live—and if so, what *is* that reason, dear heart?

Okay, let's face the fact. Like it or not, the stringer was now a guy standing on a rain-walloped parking lot in downtown Crabtown. That's all he was now. He was Tommy Moon, a Baltimore guy with very wet hair. The stringer was a 51-year-old chubster with a bald spot the size of a 50-cent piece on the crown of his rain-slopped head. Face it: he was a mouth-breather who spat flecks of white spittle whenever he talked. Too bad, huh? Moon was a loser in life's little sweepstakes—a fading little fat man who dreamed only of finding a way out of the storm.

Fight Lupus! Head lowered, he began the long trek back to the car.

2. A BULLETIN FROM CNN

The battered Chevy Sprint chugged north on Baltimore's Calvert Street. Sopping wet, the driver mulled his options.

1. Shoot yourself without delay.

2. Dull the pain inflicted by Ol' Blue Eyes with a tumbler of cheap-end vodka manufactured somewhere in small-town Indiana, or maybe in southern Ohio. Stupefy yourself with a low-priced, low-quality drinkable drug and learn to laugh again.

After vacillating between the two plans for several minutes, the stringer finally settled on No. 2. Instead of blowing his brains out, he'd pay a visit to his home-away-from-home: a low-slung, concrete edifice on 29th Street known as **BAR**.

Make no mistake: The stringer spent a great deal of his free time at **BAR**. He found major comfort there. **BAR** was a refuge from his troubled society, and from the deranged, one-eyed, blood-drunk Frankensteins who each week wrote and edited and then stapled together the garish and astonishingly tacky pages of *People* magazine.

Introducing... The 25 Sexiest People of 1995!

Make no mistake: The world's most popular feature magazine was in the grip of a dozen hypnotic-sedative addicts from the dark side of Pluto, and the stringer's only escape from the horror was **BAR**. Groaning and shivering now, he pulled the ancient Chevy onto the gravel parking lot and coasted to a stop. The engine farted twice and died. But before he could open the car door, the Nokia on the dashboard began to chatter.

Moon knew who it was without looking. "Goddam you perverted sonofabitches," growled the stringer. "Don't you ever get enough?" Yet he could not resist the electronic summons. The New York City Frankensteins owned him, after all; the stringer had child-support payments to make. And who would feed Fang his nightly, mercury-laden tuna, if the stringer didn't? Moaning with journalistic despair, he reached across the dash and snagged the infernal device. Held it to his long-suffering ear.

"Talk to me."

"Moon? This is Yang. What's the verdict?"

"Don't you ever go home, Yang?"

"I *am* home," said the Chief of the *People* Correspondent Desk, who actually ran the magazine, regardless of her formal title. "I asked you a question, putz."

"And I heard you, Iron Female. The verdict is: thumbs up. We've got ourselves a winner, Yang."

"Don't jerk me off, Moon-man."

"Hey, I would not do that. Truly. I did very well tonight… even if I didn't get the Sinatra interview, *per se*."

"*Per se*? What the fuck does that mean?"

"Well, ah… it means I wasn't able to do a full Q&A. Not yet. But we had a very good preliminary discussion, and Sinatra was very, very receptive."

"Really? I think you lie, Moon. I think you're jerking me off again, you very bad boy."

Moon sighed. (Why do men floss their gums each day? Or fail to?) "Frank wanted to know who I *was*, Yang. He asked me several times, he really did. And he listened very carefully to my questions. What an electrifying showbiz figure! What an unstoppable, inimitable, unflappable… at his age, still performing—think of it! I asked him about his amazing longevity, along with several other hard-hitting questions. Don't worry—I didn't get into his alleged mob connections or his highly dubious links to Ronald Reagan. Not at all. Why would I? What would be the point? No, sir! Frank was really intrigued, Yang; he suggested I phone his press agent next week, so we could set up a leisurely lunch. It will be just the two of us."

Yang snorted heavily. "Once again, you lie. I just *talked* to the agent, dog-breath. They threw you out of the Convention Center. Bodily. Into a driving rainstorm."

Moon sighed. "That's harsh, Yang. That's a harshly negative version of what actually took place. Our discussion was in fact quite positive. As of tonight, we're on excellent terms. And he's agreed to a 90-minute interview, sometime next week. He's agreed fully, I tell you. No subject will be off-limits—the guy loves me!"

"His gun thugs gave you the boot, you flaming baboon butt, you. They kicked your ass into the rain. Why do you lie, shithead?"

"Hey, I'm telling it like it *is*, Yang. Frank's assistants helped me find an exit after my upbeat exchange with him, that's all. They were quite gracious, quite cavalier, all things considered."

"You mean, because they didn't quickly kill you? Where are you, Moon?"

"Aah... I'm on a parking lot in northeast Baltimore." Moon gazed through the rainy windshield at the glowing neon letters he loved most: BAR.

"Are you watching CNN?"

"No, I'm not. They don't show CNN on parking lots, boss. Not yet, anyway."

"Don't smart-ass me, punk. This is fucking *Yang* you're talking to! Get your ass in front of a TV set. We've got a live one tonight, and he's right in your backyard."

"A live one?"

"A *dead* one would be more like it. A former U.S. congressman washed up on the shore of the Chesapeake Bay this afternoon. Kent Island. Do you know it?"

"Kent Island?" said Moon. "Oh, yes, I know it well. I got arrested there once, in college. Drunk and disorderly, as I recall."

"The politico's *corpus* came to rest against a fishing pier on Kent Island. A guy named Zalenka. He was a one-termer from Maryland, ten or 15 years ago. Salisbury, I think it was. Whatever. But he only held office for a couple of years. Got beat in his first re-election bid and was never heard from again."

"Right. I do remember the name. Harry Zalenka. A Democrat, I believe?"

"Correct. Very good. You're right on it."

"So what do you want from me?"

"What do I *want*? Well, Moon, it's my understanding that you work for us."

"You mean I haven't been shit-canned yet?"

"Not yet," said Yang. "But I have it on good authority that if you don't deliver that Sinatra interview soon, you're history here. Done. *Kaput*. Goodbye, yearly stringer contract. Goodbye, Moon! Did you know the Executive Editor has been threatening to dump your ass for the past six months?"

"Brickley Tolliver the Third? The big dog himself?"

"The same. Mr. Tolliver isn't very fond of you, Moon. He calls you 'Our Baltimore Asshole.'"

"Please thank him for me."

"Everybody feels very sorry for you, up here on the 37th Floor. They don't want to see you get the axe. They really don't."

"Tell them I'm grateful for their support."

"Harold G. Zalenka, aka 'Harry.' Got it? They found him at the Catch O' The Day Fishing Pier on Kent Island. Actually, he was *beneath* the pier. His corpus had bloated unfortunately, and his face had ballooned way up. Not a pretty sight, according to several witnesses. How fast can you get to Kent Island?"

"Yang, I can't go anywhere right now."

"Really? Why not?"

"I'm drenched. Soaking wet."

"Oh, that's awful. Just terrible. I can only imagine your discomfort. But time is of the essence here, Mooner. Go stand in front of a fan for 10 or 11 minutes, then get your ass moving.

Get in that crumbling ash heap you drive and light out for the territory. I want your first Zalenka file on my computer screen by noon tomorrow. Make it a *great* file, and I might be able to save your job."

Moon thought about it. He needed the dough, sorry to say. He needed the bucks. *I can't go on; I'll go on.* His life was a Beckett novel, but much darker. Bottom line: The corporate bloodsuckers at *People* had Moon by both nuts. Because he needed them in order to make his child support. And to feed his Fang. And to pay for the oceans of bottom-end vodka he downed each day. He sighed. It was the story of his life, the only life he had. "Okay, Yang, you win. Got any more on Zalenka?"

"Just a couple more things. CNN says he was living in a rundown motel in Trappe, Maryland. Nice name, huh? The Evening Breeze Motel—it's not far from Kent Island. After you check out the pier, interview everybody in the motel: the manager, the residents, the staff, you name it. I want you to go through the entire joint. Work the place like a vacuum cleaner on steroids, and don't stop until you get me something *hot.*

"Oh, and we've also got a report, just in from AP… it looks like they found Zalenka's mom. She's 86 years old, and she's a resident at the Almost Family! nursing home in northeast Baltimore. The old lady's name is Doris Zalenka. Are you writing this shit down?"

"Of course," lied Moon. "Every word you utter."

"As soon as you finish with the pier and the motel, hustle over to Almost Family! and pull a couple of tearjerker sound-bites out of Mama Z. Think you can handle that?"

"You bet I can, Yang. Tearjerker sound-bites are my forte."

"You're a real a-hole, aren't you, Moon?"

"I do my best."

The line went dead. Moon sat motionless behind the wheel for at least a minute. Then he opened the car door. The rusty hinges squealed their usual protest.

"Fuck *People*," Moon told the decaying Chevy Sprint. "And Ying Yang can kiss my hairy Irish ass—because I'm not going anywhere until I've had my hooch."

3. NO HELP FROM LIDDY

Perched on his usual barstool, the stringer hollered at the barkeep: "Hurry up, Ferguson—my *Donald*!"

Ferguson hopped to it. Two shots of "DeLuxe" vodka and half a pint of Donald Duck Orange Juice: The shit tasted like World War II-era paint thinner going down. But Moon liked the way it scalded the back of his throat. Like most former tormented Irish-Catholics who lived in fear of Screaming Hell, Moon got off on the aftertaste of decayed potatoes.

When the libation arrived, he drank deeply. And drank again. Then he shuddered, and his gut convulsed. For a precarious moment, he feared that he might actually puke. But a moment later, the anesthesia began to kick in. "Goddam, that's good," Moon croaked at the bartender. "That's my fucking *Donald*, man!"

Ferguson did not reply. Baggy-eyed and slack-mouthed, the dour Irishman was watching the TV set above the bar.

"What's the matter, Ferg? You look like you just came from a funeral."

"I did." The barkeep turned, pointed at the slowly revolving logo on the screen: *CNN Headline News*. "Didn't anybody tell you yet? We lost the Mick today."

Moon stopped guzzling his *Donald*. "Lost the Mick? *Which Mick?*"

"Mantle is gone, Tommy. The very one. Died early this morning—his fookin' liver finally gave out. Long live the Mick!"

"Oh, my God," said Moon. "Mickey Mantle. How they begged him to come off the Jack Daniels. It *was* the Jack Daniels that finished him, wasn't it?"

Ferguson nodded solemnly. "They say he drank enough JD to fill Yankee Stadium to the height of the fookin' press box. He was a giant among men, Tommy. We won't see his like again."

"Amen, and glory be, world without end." Moon waved his *Donald* in a wobbly salute. "Remember '61, and the home run battle with Maris?"

"Who could forget it, Moon?" The bartender shook his huge, tousled head. "The Mick nailed 54 that year and batted .365. The greatest fookin' slugger who ever played the game, bar none."

They fell silent after that, as CNN's half-hour news cycle started up again. Mantle was the lead story: *A Legend in Yankee Pinstripes*. "One of baseball's greatest heroes has passed away at age 63," boomed the news anchor, "his life cut tragically short by years of alcohol abuse...."

They watched a file clip of Mantle rounding the bases, after blasting a grand-slam home run at Yankee Stadium.

Then the scene slowly dissolved... to be replaced by a live report from a windswept fishing pier in Maryland.

Chrissy, I'm standing out here on the Catch O' The Day Fishing Pier at Kent Island. As you can see, it's raining pretty hard—not much visibility. According to a Coast Guard official I talked to a few minutes ago, the body of former Democratic Congressman Harry Zalenka was found wedged between two pilings, right over there at the edge of the pier. The same official said the corpse was discovered by a restaurant bus boy, and we're hoping to interview that witness shortly.

> *At this hour, no one knows why the 52-year-old Zalenka wound up floating face-down in the Chesapeake. There's also a report, so far unconfirmed, that the corpse was wearing 40 pounds of diving weights. If that's true, Zalenka may have died as the result of a scuba diving accident, since divers often wear weights on their belts for stability. And we've also been told that Zalenka's 27-foot sloop, the Razzmatazz, is missing from its slip at Turkey Point. There's speculation tonight that Zalenka might have fallen off the boat while cruising the Chesapeake during the past few days. Meanwhile, State Police sources tell us the congressman's body has been transported to the Maryland Medical Examiner's Office for autopsy, pending notification of kin.*

Moon watched the report carefully, then called for another *Donald*. He took a deep hit and waited for his second buzz. *A drowned congressman and a missing sailboat. And the corpse washes ashore wearing 40 pounds of scuba weights?* A diving accident? Foul play? Or had the driftwood-politician actually ended his own life by jumping from the boat while wearing a belt full of lead? Had Zalenka tried to make his suicide look like an accidental drowning… maybe in order to protect a big life insurance payoff?

Questions, questions.

It was time for a reality check.

"Back in a minute, Ferg—gotta hit the can."

Standing alone in the dim hallway that flanked the pisser, Moon tapped a familiar phone number into his cell. The green digits flickered, then flashed away as the call went racing through.

"Liddy here. What?"

"G. Gordon? Hey, it's Tommy Moon."

Liddy groaned. "Oh, shit. You, again? The answer is *no*."

"Fair enough. What's the question?"

"The question is: Got any inside dope on the congressman who just went for a swim in the Chesapeake?"

"You're right, G. That *is* the question."

"I thought so. And you just heard my answer."

"Why do I have trouble believing you, G. Gordon?"

"Don't fuck with me, Moon. Remember what I told you the first time we met?"

"I do."

"What was it?"

"You noted for the record that you could kill me with an ordinary No. 2 pencil in less than one second. You said you could easily insert it into my eyeball and then punch it straight through my brain. Death would be instantaneous."

"That's correct. Good recall!" The infamous Watergate burglar produced a subterranean growl—probably an attempt at a laugh, but you could never be sure. "Keep that scenario in mind, dogmeat."

"I will, G. The concept is easy to remember."

"Anything else, Moon? I'm very busy here."

"I'm asking for your gut reaction, G. The vibe, you know? Did Zalenka fall off his own poop-deck by accident? Or did some bad people put him in the water and then set his boat adrift, so it would look like an accident?"

The cat burglar sent up a derisive snort. "How the fuck should I know? Am I the gypsy lady?"

"You're the smartest former White House dark-side burglar in Washington, are you not?"

"That's correct."

"Well, isn't that the sort of thing a really smart former White House dark-side burglar *ought* to know?"

Liddy emitted a deep, oily chuckle. "Before I answer your question, I've got one of my own."

"Ask it."

"When is that shitrag of yours gonna run my profile?"

Moon blinked. Fast. "Oh, *that*. Any day now. Could be next week! They've already closed the story I wrote, G. It's been edited and fact-checked and proofed—the works. They're just waiting for a hole in the *Up Front* section. Won't be long now, my man. It's a done deal, trust me."

"Waiting for a hole, are they? In the *Up Front* section? Why don't I feel convinced, Moon?"

"I'm not sure why. You tell me."

"Maybe it's because of the way you've been stringing me along for six months now, you lying sack of shit. Week after week, I run to the corner newsstand, and no feature on the G Man. It's fucking humiliating, you double-dealing little shit!"

Moon closed his eyes. "Gordon, Gordon. That story is *happening*, man. It's going over the top. Honest to God, it's already been laid out. A three-page spread—I've seen the art myself. The lead photo has you in the candy-apple Corvette, and we can read the *h2o-Gate* license plate loud and clear. The editors say they're thrilled, absolutely thrilled with this one. Great story! That's all I'm hearing out of New York: Great story!"

"Right. And I'll be eating spaghetti with the Pope at the Vatican tonight." The freelance surveillance guru cut loose with another sarcastic guffaw. "You tell me these things, Moon. You tell me these fabulous things, day after day, but the profile never *runs*. Six months I'm waiting. And I do need that story to run. It will help sell copies of my next book."

"You've got another one in the pipeline?"

"Sure do. Haven't you heard? Putnam is bringing it out. *Liddy: Inside the Soul of a True American Patriot*. It will hit the stands late next month. I'm already booked on *Larry King Live*."

"Congratulations, G. Nice work, as always."

"Thank you, as always. Are we done now?"

"Not quite. Gordon, I asked you once and I'll ask you again: If the body of a former U.S. Congressman washes ashore, and if that body happens to be wearing 40 pounds of diving-weights, what do these facts suggest?"

"You mean, in an existential sense? They suggest fate. Destiny. Nietzsche. The Monster of Energy."

"Really? That's pretty deep, G. How about in a *criminological* sense? As in: Who dun it?"

"Oh, *that*. Probably a suicide."

"Really? You think he killed himself?"

"Sure. Why not? He cried out in despair: 'Goodbye, cruel world.' Then he jumped off his boat, and it drifted away. They haven't found it yet, but I bet they will."

"And the diving weights? Maybe he went scuba-diving and had an accident?"

"Naah. He took himself out, Moon. He put those weights around his belt because he wanted to stay down, probably for insurance reasons. If he disappears forever, remember, they gotta pay the family. But if he floats back up—*Hey, look at me!*—there might be troubling legal questions. Maybe no big payday for the beneficiaries."

Moon ruminated. "I don't know. It doesn't feel right, Gordon."

Liddy groaned. "Knock off the melodrama, dimwit. Who are you, John Le Carre? Stop complicating matters. Trust me: They'll find his abandoned sailboat in a few days, drifting aimlessly. He jumped, that's all. The guy strapped on the diving weights and went in the water. Sayonara! Wait and see."

Moon frowned. Shook his head. "I'm not buying, Gordon. You've got some inside skinny on this thing—I can feel it."

"That's ridiculous."

"Bullshit. You *know* something, renowned cat burglar."

"Not true. I'm dumb as Ronald Reagan on this one. Don't have a clue. Only know what I see on Dan Rather at 6:30 p.m."

"Somebody took Zalenka out, didn't they?"

Liddy sighed. "Good night, Moon. I'll be watching for that profile. Can't wait to see how I look in the Corvette."

"Wait a minute, don't hang up. I'm going to need you in the next few days, Gordon. Gonna need your input—I've just been assigned to cover the story for *People*."

"Really? I'm sorry to hear it; Zalenka deserved better. Besides, I want you working on *my* story, not his."

"G., you have my word. Your story is happening, man. It will be a major publishing event. The talk shows will be screaming for you. Will you please buzz me when you get the lowdown on Zalenka?"

"Fuck, no. I certainly won't."

"Thank you, Gordon."

Followed by the dial tone.

Returning to his stool, the stringer finished his *Donald*, then launched a ten-spot toward the bar. "I hate to leave you, Fergie, but it's time to go."

The burly barkeep glared at him. "You're going home at eleven p.m.? You're not closing the joint? I can't believe this."

"Duty calls," said Moon. "I'm working a story early in the morning. An investigative special for *People*."

Ferguson rumbled with subterranean laughter. "Investigative reporting for *People*? What... *Inside Julia Roberts' Amazing New Hair-Do?*"

"Not exactly. A political saga this time. Cloak and dagger stuff, you bet." He took a long look at the gloomy-eyed giant behind the bar. "Listen, Ferg, how's your younger brother doing these days?"

The bartender brightened. "Little Billy? He's going good. Doing just fine. He's off the peppermint schnapps and he's been attending meetings again, one day at a time. 'One drink's too many, and a thousand drinks ain't enough.' That's my bro—a one-man AA meeting! Keep your fingers crossed."

"Still chasing bad guys for the Bureau, is he?"

"You better believe it," said Ferguson. Now he was standing tall, standing proud, with his shoulders snapped back at full attention. "FBI Special Agent William Cooley Ferguson—and Little Billy always gets his man—provided he stays sober, that is." It was the first time the sullen barkeep had smiled that night.

"Give him my best, then," said Moon. "Good night, Ferg."

The big man nodded. "Good night, Mooner. Stay dry."

4. AT THE DUMP

Home again, home again. And welcome to The Dump!

As he stumbled into his one-room hideout on Porthole Alley—a narrow strip of brick row-houses that flanked the seediest section of the Baltimore waterfront—Moon's right foot came into contact with an economy-size can of Bumblebee Tuna. The can shot across the floorboards like a runaway hockey puck and plowed into a plump fur-ball that was dozing in front of the midget refrigerator.

Meeeeee...*yowwwwcch*! With a snarl of rage, the fur-ball sprang onto all fours, hackles bristling.

"Sorry, Fang," said Moon. "That was purely accidental, I swear it."

Fang did not reply, but stood motionless and glaring, defending his space. He was a Maine Coon, one of the largest American felines, with the huge green eyes and the grotesquely bulging gut of a gone-to-fat Sumo wrestler.

For ten seconds, they confronted each other in silence. Moon was the first to speak. "I'm warning you, Fang; I've had a very difficult evening." He made a fist with his right hand and shook it. "Sinatra pissed all over me and then a dead congressman washed ashore. And I drew the assignment. And to top it all off, the Mick is dead—the fucking *Mick*! Give me the slightest bit of shit, and I'll lock your ass in the basement dryer again. I'll hit the 'Spin' button, Fang, I swear it. Remember the last time we did that?"

The cat groaned from somewhere deep in his voice box. It was the sound fear makes, building within.

"That's better," said Moon. "Now get over to your feed bowl and stand at attention."

Eyeing him warily, Fang inched toward the center of the room... where Moon was already digging through a pile of dirty laundry in search of the can opener. He fumbled for at least a minute, then struck gold: *gotcha*! Working swiftly, he attached the cutting edge to the Bumblebee can and started cranking. Fang recognized the sound instantly, and his tawny eyes lit up with the usual disgusting greed. Moon dumped the fish flesh into a bowl marked *Fang's Repast*, then dropped the can and stepped over the laundry pile to the plastic coffee table.

Between two overflowing ashtrays, the red light on the answering machine was flashing *1-2-3, 1-2-3*.

Already unbuttoning his damp shirt with one hand, he hit the "Message" button with the other. He could hear Fang slobbering in the background as he ripped through the defenseless tuna. The first message was one he'd been expecting for several days: "Mr. Moon, would you please call the Baltimore Department of Streets and Traffic Fines Division immediately? This is your final notice, sir. Continuing failure to remit your $327.50 in back fines and penalties will result in the immediate impoundment of your vehicle."

"Right," said the stringer. "You bet. Did you hear that, Fang? They want to impound the Sprint. Hey, they can bite my *wazonga*, whaddya say to that, Wild Thing?"

The cat slobbered on, oblivious.

The second message also failed to lift his spirits. It was from Yang, who'd called 60 minutes earlier, while he was visiting BAR. "Moon, do you think I'm a fucking idiot? I know goddam right well you didn't go to Kent Island tonight. You're in that shithole Fenian bar of yours again, swilling cut-rate vodka and talking up the IRA. Well, I'm warning you right now: If you get drunk and vanish on me, you're finished at *People*. I want you on that pier at sunup, cowboy!"

But the last message was the toughest one of all. It had come in a little before midnight. "Dad? This is Keera. If you're there, will you pick up?" A long pause, while she waited. Then: "Hey, I'm looking forward to the movies on Tuesday. Listen, we need to talk. Mom's new boyfriend gave me all this shit...."

He heard her sob once. Then she caught herself. With forced brightness: "See you Tuesday, Dad!"

By now Fang had retreated to his crap-out space in front of the midget fridge, where he would soon launch his usual loathsome burping routine. The stringer stood motionless in the kitchen for two or three minutes, thinking. Then he opened the refrigerator door and gazed upon the contents. They included a wax paper-wrapped dill pickle from the 23rd Street Deli, a plastic container of Redi-Whip Dessert Topping, a nearly empty package of prehistoric bacon and a cardboard carryout box of two-day-old *General Pao's Szechuan Chicken*.

The stringer carried the carton over to the window. He set it down and went back to the sink, where he retrieved a wet spoon and wiped it clean on his pants leg. Returning to the window, he sat down on the metal folding chair. He ate the remains of *General Pao* slowly, while rain fell through the streetlight outside his window.

MONDAY

1. CROSS YANG,
AND DIE YOUNG

Dawn. The Atlantic monsoon had departed during the night, and the dawn broke in a flood of streaming, golden sunshine.

Moon slept through the light show, however. He also slept through seven o'clock, eight o'clock and nine. When his eyes finally snapped open, they went first to the digital clock on the bedside table. The clock said: *9:14*.

"Aw, *fuck*!"

He leapt from the sofa bed and landed squarely on Fang's left forepaw. Once again the cat screamed at him: "Meee-*yowwwch*!" Teeth bared, the enraged feline feinted once toward Moon's exposed shins, then skulked off to nurse his bruises. Moon began struggling to pull on last night's still damp socks... even as he offered a series of futile apologies to his miffed roommate. "Hey, fella, I'm sorry, okay? It was an accident. Get over it, will you?"

But the cat refused to meet his eye.

"I said it was *unintentional*, you unforgiving sonofabitch!"

No response. Awash in irrational guilt, Moon hustled across the room and flung open the midget refrigerator door. Desperate to make amends, he snagged the mold-crusted pack of bacon and tore the plastic wrapper away. Then he flung the raw pork toward the offended brute's lair. "Eat up, you heartless bastard. Clog your arteries and die of bacon-stroke—what the hell do I care?"

He slammed the door behind him, and 30 seconds later he was climbing into the Sprint. He turned the key, and got nothing for three or four seconds. Then the starter screamed like a tormented banshee. And died. He turned the key... more nothing. *Please, please...* and at last the engine caught and held. (Years and years ago, Moon had stopped asking: *Why is everything so fucking hard for me? Why is my life a sadist's torture pit?* Questions, questions.)

Nursing the accelerator carefully, he eased out of the parking space, and the Sprint crept slowly forward. He held his breath while the engine bucked and jerked, then backfired angrily. It was touch and go for a few more seconds... but at last the ruckus quieted and he was able to join the traffic flowing south toward the Jones Falls Expressway.

Nine-thirty, already.

Yang was going to fry his ass.

But the stringer needed black coffee. Needed it bad. Still cursing and muttering, he whipped the prehistoric car into the 7-Eleven at Howard and 27th. The cashier—a surly, tattooed Filipino in plastic flip-flops and a dayglo-orange Baltimore Orioles cap—rang up Moon's 12-ounce cup of java and then went back to leafing through his *Axe-Murderer Magazine.*

Ah yes, life in the city.

He took 95 south to the exit for *BAY BRIDGE & EASTERN SHORE.* The sun was well up in the sky now, and doing its best to burn off the brownish haze rising from the Eastside Trash Incinerator. More than a decade before, health experts from nearby Johns Hopkins University had announced that the incinerator smog caused bone cancer. By now at least a dozen studies had shown that the bone cancer rate on the east side of the city was triple the national rate. But the lucrative incinerator was owned and operated by one of the mayor's closest political cronies and campaign fundraisers, so the poisoning went on without letup, day after day. And thus the local *mantra* continued, from one year to the next: "We're all being fucked up the butt for profit here, and nobody can hope to resist. Bend over and spread those cheeks—this is *Baltimore*, kemo sabe!"

Forward, march. Groaning with anxiety—*I've really done it, this time*—Moon put the speedometer needle on 72 and tried to keep an eye out for the black-and-gold cruisers of the Maryland State Police. He was making good time... but what about his tires? He was riding on shit, and he knew it. How many times had that mechanic on Harford Road warned him: "Replace those losers now, or die soon in a fiery crash"?

Moaning fretfully, the stringer prayed his endless, desperate prayer: *Dear Lord—but not a British Lord—please protect me where the rubber meets the road!*

Onward. The tires held somehow and within a matter of minutes he was zooming up an elevated ramp toward the towering steel colossus that was the Chesapeake Bay Bridge. The center span loomed 340 feet above the electric-blue waters of the great estuary, and the view from here was nothing less than spectacular. From this lofty perch, you couldn't tell that vast sections of the gorgeous waterway—starved for oxygen by billions of gallons of illegal industrial runoff—had been declared "dead zones" by conservation officials and were now completely devoid of marine life.

But Moon had no time to mourn the Bay's imminent demise, or even to ogle the wheeling gulls and the distant, toy-like oil tankers from Riyadh. Moon was late, and his paltry paycheck hung in the balance. *Move it! Fried ass!*

Like the other hapless stringers who worked for *People* (about 150 of them, all told), Moon lived in total fear of Yang Yang. And for good reason: Yang was a ruthless, boxcutter-wielding Taiwanese bitch. Push that heartless Chink too far, and she'd cut your balls off so quickly you'd never even feel the blade. The truth was, she ran the entire magazine from her tiny cubicle on the 37th floor. How she managed this feat was a great mystery, since her informal title—"Stringer Chief"— told you almost nothing about her actual role among the Time Warner moguls who masterminded the magazine.

Yang was a tiny creature, only four feet, eleven inches tall. But her narrow face was a frozen hatchet, and her laser-eyes could slice through the toughest steel. Yang gave the orders at

People, and everybody on the magazine fully understood the drill. Only the executive editor, the Yale-educated Brickley Tolliver III, had the power to countermand her directives, if he dared. But "Tolliver One-Two-Three" (as he was known to the army of *People* stringers) preferred to remain invisible for the most part... while leaving his Asian assassin to dictate coverage and story-play from her invincible redoubt near the top of the editorial food chain.

Cross Yang, and die young: That was the reality at *People*. And what had she told Moon only the night before? "I want that Zalenka file on my desk by noon tomorrow, or else!"

Sixteen minutes after crossing the bridge, Moon's panting Sprint reached the brine-lapped precincts of Kent Island. Three minutes after that, he was parking the car and running toward the sun-bright pine planks of the Catch O' The Day Pier. But it was a pointless quest, and he knew it. Once again, he'd snored through cutting-edge developments; his story had moved on several hours ago.

There was nothing to report here... except for the quaint (and thoroughly useless) fact that several of the retirees who fished the pier daily were "catchin' some damn nice croaker on cut squid!"

Moon spent exactly eight minutes on the pier, during which he asked half a dozen tottering croaker-catchers: "Heard anything about the dead congressman?"

"Yassir. Sure did. Poor bastard washed up right under this pier. Late yesterday afternoon, it was. Hell of a thing. *Hell* of a thing. They took the body away just before sunset is what I heard."

"That sounds about right. Did you see any cops or Coast Guard around here?"

"Yassir, they was here a while, but they all gone now. There was two State *Po*-lice and a Coast Guard guy here until about 45 minutes ago. Too bad you got here so late—they all done taken off on you. You coulda interviewed them boys and gotten some *good* stuff. But now you're stuck!"

"That's true," said Moon. "I'm totally stuck." (While thinking: *You redneck-bozerino—I'd like to set fire to your hair.*)

Screwed! There was no cure for it but to head for The Evening Breeze Motel over in Trappe, and try to scare up some interviews in the dead man's former neighborhood.

Fried ass! He hustled back to his sweltering vehicle (the air conditioner had expired years ago) and headed east on Rte. 50 towards the motel. His first stringer file for "Zalenkadrown" (the file-name, or "slug," he'd be using from here on, as the story coverage unfolded) was due in exactly 10 minutes, and so far he hadn't interviewed even a single news source.

Move over, Harry, he muttered to the shade of the kaput congressman. *I'm every bit as dead as you are.*

2. DEAD MAN'S MOTEL, TRAPPE

The Evening Breeze was a vision straight out of Dante: 14 peeling cabins, turd-brown, high above which loomed a burned-out neon sign: *Free HBO!* In the stark light of noon-time, the cabins threw black-edged shadows so sharp they hurt the eye. On the far side of the motel, a thousand acres of ripe soybeans blazed emerald-green all the way to the horizon. *Give up all hope, ye who enter here!*

Approaching the door of Unit No. Six, Zalenka's former abode, the stringer was distressed to find a tall gentleman blocking his path. The gentleman wore a dark suit, mirror sunglasses and a flesh-colored radio plug in one ear. A royal-blue tag dangled from his tie: *FBI Special Agent Floyd Murchison.*

Now the gentleman glared. "Can I help you, sir?"

"Yes, sir, you can," said Moon. "And I thank you for it." He pointed toward No. Six. "I need to go in that motel room."

"Do you? And why would that be?"

"I'm covering the Zalenka story."

"For who?"

"For *People.*"

"*People* Magazine?" The Special Agent cocked an eyebrow. "I thought you guys only chased movie stars. Along with Princess Di and Oprah Winfrey, of course."

Ignoring the jibe, Moon simply held up his plastic Time Warner I.D. "I do thank you for your help, officer."

The Special Agent grinned at him. There were pale, washed-out freckles scattered all across the lawman's forehead, and the mirror sunglasses flashed ominously. In spite of his neatly pressed suit and tie, he looked like a small-town Texas mass murderer on a three-week crystal meth binge. "Oh, I'm not an *officer*," he said with a chuckle now. "I'm an FBI Special Agent, and this is a federal crime scene—so there's no news media permitted. I already ran off a guy from the Washington *Post*."

"A crime scene? What crime are we talking about, Agent Murchison?"

"It's a potential homicide, Mr. Moon. We've got an unexplained death here, and the deceased is a former federal elected official."

Moon nodded. "So what makes you think it was homicide?"

The Special Agent pushed the sunglasses down lower on his nose and scowled angrily. "I didn't say I *thought* it was a homicide, Mr. *People*. I said 'potential' homicide. It's an unexplained death, that's all." He squinted through the high-noon glare at his interrogator, and his eyes widened slowly as he realized his mistake. "Hey, you're not planning to *quote* me, are you?"

"Why not?" Moon shrugged. "That was a pretty good sound-bite, Agent Murchison: 'It's a potential homicide; we've got an unexplained death here.'"

The Special Agent's mouth narrowed down to an angry slit. "Wait a minute. You know goddam right well that comment was off the record!"

"Was it? I don't remember discussing that aspect before you spoke."

Murchison's glare was solid ice. "You..."

"Sonofabitch," Moon finished the sentence for him. "Hey, I tell you what: I'll be perfectly happy to keep your remarks off the record… in return for five minutes in that motel room. You have my word."

The Special Agent gnawed at his gum for a few seconds, while his blue eyes radiated sweet-pure Texas hatred. "Okay… but the fuckin' clock is running, pal. You got exactly five minutes before I come in there after you."

"Fair deal," said Moon. "And I do thank you, Special Agent."

"The clock is running, fart-face."

The Special Agent stepped aside, and the stringer pushed open the screen door. A moment later he was stepping into the gloom of Number Six.

3. HELP FROM LITTLE DEBBIE

First impression: The smell. *The dead always leave their animal smell behind.* The aroma was strongest near the bed, on which the Bureau had dumped *Zalenkadrown's* clothes. Moon eyeballed mouse-gray Fruit-of-the-Loom, a frayed sweatshirt, ratty sneakers. He walked slowly around the mess. A few dirty socks, rolled into balls. An empty half-pint container of *Dairy Maid* chocolate milk. Moon looked but did not touch. He stood motionless beside the bed, staring at a torn tee shirt, its underarms stained yellow with ancient perspiration.

That animal smell.

My heart is heavy, the stringer told himself. *I hope this isn't clinical depression.* Moon had seen a lot of death during his years as a journalist, but he'd never gotten used to it. He'd covered plane crashes and train wrecks and earthquakes that had crumpled entire villages like stacked cartons of stomped-on eggs. He'd stood beside walls that dribbled the oozy brain matter of shotgun suicides, and on a couple of occasions, he'd peered into closets where the victims of mass executions sat crowded together like dazed airline passengers after a coast-to-coast flight. Once, he'd even helped a Baltimore homicide detective search for bullet-scattered teeth along a dimly lit hallway.

But that animal smell? He'd never gotten used to it.

Sighing, he stepped away from the bed and moved across the linoleum toward the kitchenette. He stood in front of the sink, studying the dripping spigot, the maroon countertop. He noted the discarded pie box—a Little Debbie "Personal Pie"— with the brown ants crawling through it. Had this been the dead man's last sad, small meal on *terra firma,* before boarding the *Razzmatazz* for his date with death?

Maybe.

He eyeballed the little box, the freckled redhead beaming from its side. Little Debbie.

French apple. It was a "personal pie."

My heart is heavy. Leaning on the sink, he watched a line of ants marching toward the scattered pie crumbs. One of the insects had managed to strip a grain of sugar from the pasteboard; now he lugged it slowly along the countertop. Bringing it back to the nest, was he? The stringer felt a great weariness descending upon his brain. He turned to stare through the single window. On the other side of the dusty plate glass, greenripe soybeans ran on as far as the eye could reach, dozed fitfully beneath the hot white eye of the August sun.

Then a grasshopper appeared on the window screen. The creature's mouth-parts gleamed like polished metal in the beating glare. The stringer noted the wet tobacco-slobber lapping against the screen. *He's hungry, too. He wants a piece of Little Debbie for himself.*

What could Moon learn from this motel room? Could this room teach him anything? Tan carpet… worn through in spots. Cinderblock floor beneath. Walls of lumpy, shit-brown stucco. Window air conditioner, *Trane,* gurgling like a terminal patient on a respirator. And the pie box sitting on the counter. About the size of a deck of cards. Little Debbie. The stringer yawned—he felt such lassitude—and then, acting on the merest whim, he reached over and picked up the little carton.

And got a mild surprise.

Someone had scribbled a few letters on the countertop. With the pie box out of the way, they were plainly revealed. Black letters… probably scrawled in haste with a felt-tip pen.

SAMSA.

That was all. Five black letters in caps: SAMSA. Moon examined them. A clue? A name? Perhaps the acronym for some exotic and obscure government bureaucracy? He stared at the letters. Maybe the *Strategic Agency for Mapping, Surveying & Analysis?* Or how about: *Satellite Administration, Maritime Systems Assessment?*

Whatever. The five letters meant nothing to Moon, but he copied them down for the record and then replaced the pie box. He wondered: Had the Bureau gumshoes seen those black markings when they tossed the room? Would they mean anything more to the FBI than they meant to him? SAMSA...

Had *Zalenkadrown* scrawled that single word on the countertop before setting sail on the final journey aboard the *Razzmatazz*?

Questions, questions. But then a shadow fell in the doorway. "Let's go, buster-boy—the game-clock just hit zero."

Moon stepped away from the sink.

"Give me one more minute, will you?" The Special Agent nodded but remained in the doorway. Moving quickly, the stringer inventoried the rest of the unit. He noted the rattletrap Zenith portable TV atop the clothes dresser... the four wire coat hangers hanging in the tiny closet. The worn-out toothbrush and the mini-tube of Pepsodent in the crapper. The Gideon Bible stashed inside the top drawer of the otherwise empty writing table.

Nothing. The FBI had done its work carefully, as always, and they'd obviously taken everything of interest with them. But had they spotted the writing on the countertop? SAMSA...

He was moving toward the door. At six-three, Murchison loomed high above the dumpy, balding stringer. "The poor bastard," said Moon. He slowed his step. "Reduced to living in a shithole like this... and then he falls off his own rundown sailboat. What a way to go."

The gentleman in the silver-striped tie laughed out loud. "Come on, Clark Kent. Nobody said he fell off his boat. Do you think I'm stupid? Hey, I'm not about to confirm the cause of death for you, Mr. *People*."

"Understood," said Moon. He was watching Murchison carefully. "Okay, instead of asking you for a news tip, I'll give you one. Did you know this guy worked for SAMSA?"

No reaction. Murchison didn't move. The mirror lenses flashed once and then dulled as the sun went behind a cloud. "I have no idea what you're referring to, sir. And I'm not going to comment. We don't talk about ongoing investigations, period. And we haven't. You know that. We've never even met, you and me."

"Correct," said the stringer. "That's one hundred percent correct. As a matter of fact, I don't even know your name. I've already forgotten it."

"That's the way I like it," grinned the Special Agent. "No name, and no fame." He removed the glasses slowly, and smiled. Then he blinked at the stringer with his flat dead eyes. "Listen, you have yourself a really nice day."

4. LUNCH WITH SPIDER

He went slowly down the line of motel units, knocking on doors and asking the occupants if they'd ever talked to "the gentleman in Number Six." He tried every door at The Evening Breeze, and he got nowhere fast.

Unit #5: "You mean the dead guy on CNN?" asks the chunky blonde in the blue *Wendy's* smock. "He kept to himself, pretty much. People here at the Breeze... they don't know their neighbors. He seemed pleasant enough, and I'm sorry he's dead. Anything else? I'm in transition here myself."

Unit #7: "What're you peddling, bud?" "Nothing." "Bullshit." "Nope, I'm just a reporter. Did you happen to know the guy who lived next door? Harry Zalenka?" "You a cop? I don't like cops." The door slams shut in his face.

Unit #8: "You bettah stop bangin' on these doors, sweetheart," wails the elderly black woman in the purple head-rag. "You keep on bangin', you goin' get yo ass *shot!*"

Nothing. Moon was running out of motel cabins. Drifting along the gravel driveway that ringed the units, he watched a gray seagull riding the air currents above the soybeans. The gull was hungry, too; his beady eyes were scanning the green leaves like radar. He was hunting grasshoppers. The stringer remembered the tobacco-slobber on the screen. *Reality 101: Everything here eats something else. Or soon dies.*

He rapped the knuckles of his right hand against the door of Unit #9. Silence. He rapped again. Silence. He was about to turn away when a muffled voice said: "Just push the fucker on open."

"Pardon?"

"I said, push the goddam door open! Are you deaf?"

Moon pushed. Sure enough, the latch gave easily and the battered door swung inwards, revealing an unusual sight. A skinny old man in a pair of bright red walking shorts and nothing else sat at a rickety-looking card table eating from a cardboard box marked *Taco Bell*.

"Well, shit, look what the wind blew in! Haw! Hey, you want a bean *burrito*?" Grinning happily, the geezer held out a greasy slab of fried corn stuffed with ground meat and beans. "Just what the doctor ordered, *ranchero*."

"Thank you, no," said Moon. "I ate already."

The older man nodded, then chewed. "You with that FBI guy out there? Jesus, I hope not. I don't like those mirror sunglasses of his—sonofabitch looks like he should be runnin' a chain gang."

Moon shook his head. "No, sir. I'm not with the Bureau. I'm a stringer for *People* magazine. I'm working the Zalenka story. I've been asking the folks here at the motel about your former neighbor, the guy who used to live in Number Six."

"Harry Zalenka?" The geezer was squinting hard at him. "You mean Mr. Total Fuckup? I could write a book about that sorry-ass loser if I wanted to."

Moon nodded. "I wish you would. I know I'd read it. Can I ask you a couple of questions, sir?"

The shirtless man burped loudly, then swallowed. He looked half-starved, with thin sticks for ribs and a tangled *Brillo* pad of gray hair at the center of his chest. He wore a bright red *Phillies* baseball cap tilted way back on his head. His features were sharp, angular—and Moon quickly noted two other distinguishing marks: a ragged scar that ran across the bridge of his nose and a prominent brown mole that rode his upper lip. "You can ask me anything you want, sonny," the old geezer piped now in a high-pitched voice that reminded Moon of the seagulls on patrol around the motel, "as long as you ain't law enforcement. Sure you ain't a cop?"

"I am."

"Then sit your ass down. You can watch *me* eat." The gray-beard dropped his *burrito* and reached for some napkins. When his hands were clean, he extended one toward the stringer. "Shake hands with the Spider, son."

"The Spider?" Moon took the hand. It was warm and oily; apparently, the napkins had missed a spot.

"Well, that's just my nickname: Spider. My real handle's George Yarnell, age 68 and at your service." The beady eyes swiveled around the room, then returned to Moon. "Say, can you put me into that magazine of yours? Can you quote me a little bit and make me look like I know what I'm talkin' about? I got a little honey I want to impress. She reads *People* every week. You quote me some, it might help me get in her pants."

"Sure," said Moon. "I can do that. Absolutely."

"Can you put me on the cover?"

"Maybe," lied Moon. "Why not? Provided you help us with some details about Zalenka, that is. You say you knew him a little bit, is that right? How long?"

"Long enough, sonny, long enough. That sad asshole tried to drag me into his craziness, but I jumped clear." Yarnell chuckled, then slurped on the straw in his Pepsi. "I'm like a spider that way. It's how I got my nickname—jumping like a spider. Anybody tries to fuck with me, I jump clear." He stared at Moon for a moment. "Did you know your average spider can jump fifty times farther than your average human, all things being equal?"

"Nope," said Moon. "Never heard that."

"It's true. Fifty times. Your ordinary garden spider could run rings around the best point-guard in the NBA. All things being equal, of course."

Moon thought about it. "That's very interesting. They must have powerful legs. But what about Zalenka? What was he like? As a person, I mean?"

The older man snickered, then set down his bean sandwich. "I can tell you for a fact that Harry Zalenka was a deeply, deeply troubled man. Do you know what a wet brain is, son?"

"No, sir. I don't."

"Okay. A wet brain is a drunk whose mind had died. He's so far gone, you gotta swaddle him in diapers before he can go out in public. He's nothing more than a vegetable that shits itself. Am I clear? Well, Harry Zalenka was well on his way to wet brain status. Okay? He used to sit over there in Number Six all day long, drinking malt liquor and listening to Roy Orbison tapes. Do you know *Only the Lonely?*"

"I do."

"Harry must've listened to *Only the Lonely* ten thousand times. He was one pathetic misfit, lemme tell you."

"I see."

"Do you?" Spider was squinting at him again. "Harry was a human train wreck, mister, and I guess he derailed right here at the Last Resort Motel. I'm talking about burning boxcars and twisted metal, *compadre*. Total human wreckage, if you catch my drift? His wife dumped him five or six years ago, and his grown-up kids wanted no part of him, either. There's a saying in AA: 'One drink's too many, and a thousand drinks ain't enough."

"Yes, I've heard that saying."

"Poor Harry. He wouldn't listen to me. I warned him. I did. I begged him to go to meetings. But he wouldn't do it. He was damaged goods, that's all. And he was living in the past. 'Spider,' he'd tell me after a few pops, 'I was hot shit up on Capitol Hill. I was once a leading member of the U.S. Congress, believe it or not!'

"Pretty goddam pathetic, huh?" The old man groaned and shook his head. "I thought he was full of shit at first. I said, 'Ain't no way this crazy smoke-hound ever served in Congress.' But then he showed me all these clippings he had in a beat-up old briefcase. Pretty impressive, you bet. But that was fifteen years ago, and he fell apart after that. By the time I met him—here at the No-Tell Motel—Harry was just another fading lush. I think the poor bastard was probably lucky, drowning in the Bay like he did."

The stringer stopped writing in his notebook. "Why do you say that?"

"Didn't I just tell you he was headed for the wet brain warehouse? He'd have ended up in Pampers, barking at the moon. This way, at least he went out quick."

Moon thought for a moment. "Spider... you called him 'crazy' just now. Are you saying he had, like, strange ideas?"

"You better believe it, hoss. Harry was one strange ranger, for certain. Like... he was full of conspiracies, okay? Who really killed JFK? Who really killed *MLK*? Bobby Kennedy—how come there were more bullets fired at Bobby Kennedy than there were bullets in that Arab fucker's gun?'"

Yarnell paused, then chewed for a minute. "How can I put this across to you? See... Harry believed the federal government had been taken over by some kind of invisible conspiracy."

Moon looked at the bare-chested man beside the card table, at the *burrito* mess in front of him. Once again, he recalled the grasshopper on the screen. Recalled his tobacco-slobber. *Everything here eats something else.* "An invisible conspiracy, Spider? Was he talking about the Capitol Hill lobbyists, do you think? An alien force like that, bent on destruction for its own purposes?"

Yarnell leaned back in his chair and burped again. He was obviously enjoying himself. "Yeah, that's it—an alien force! See how crazy he was? Shit, everybody knows the only alien force at work in Washington is the Democratic Party. Haw!

"If you ask me, his trouble started way back when he first worked in Washington. Back in the early 1980s. He saw some dirty shit as a congressman, and he started losing his grip. You know, them politicians run up against a lot of dark stuff. They see the dregs. I think the corruption must've preyed on his mind. Eventually, it must've drove him over the edge. He grabbed the hooch-bottle and tried to climb inside."

Moon deliberated. "Did he tell you about the corruption, Spider?"

"He sure did, pal. Told me about payoffs where high-ranking people in the White House and Congress were collecting big piles of cash in paper bags. He said political extortion was the order of the day—there was a regular fee schedule, if you wanted something tacked onto a bill. He said he knew of all-night orgies where U.S. senators were snortin' coke and getting it on with 16-year-old girls—and boys.

"Nasty, huh?" The old man took another slug of his fizz-drink. "And there was more. He said there was treachery running loose all over the government. He believed there was a mole. That's the word he used. He'd get half-lit, and then he'd start in on it: 'Spider, there's a mole way up high in the CIA.'"

Moon had stopped writing by now. "A mole? You mean… a foreign spy?"

"You're fucking-a, a foreign spy." The old man paused in order to dip a chunk of *taco* into a paper cup of *guacamole*. "Zalenka would get mad as hell, and he'd start yelling at me: 'There's a Soviet mole on the loose, giving away our secrets! Giving away our satellite secrets! He gave the Russians Big Bird, and he's gotta be stopped!'"

"Big Bird?"

"Satellite system. Spy in the sky, you know? Zalenka told me it was state of the art—with video cameras so good they could tell what brand of cigarettes you're smoking, from 300 miles out in space. Like I told you, he was crazy as bat shit. What you planning to write about him, anyway?"

"Don't know yet," said the stringer. "I'm still trying to figure out who he was, really, and what happened to him."

Yarnell snorted. "Well, shit, I've told you plenty, and you're free to use all of it. But let's back up a minute: what I want to know is, can you put me on the cover of your magazine? I want to impress my little honey."

Moon was rubbing his eyes. "It's a maybe, Spider, but I'll do my best. We'll have to see how the story plays out. Can you think of anybody else I might talk to… anybody who could give us more detail?"

Spider deliberated. "Well, Harry did have one friend who dropped by the motel now and then to gab with him. This fat criminal lawyer from over in Pocomoke City. Melvin Fishpaw is his name. You ever heard of him? He's 300 pounds easy. Gigantic ass on him. And shabby as all hell… a real sleaze-bag. But Zalenka said Fishpaw was a big deal in Washington.

'Take my word for it, Spider—Melvin Fishpaw's working at the highest levels of our federal government!' Haw! What a joke. A great big sack of blubber like that?"

Sighing and shaking his head, the old man had begun to stuff his food wrappers into the *Taco Bell* box. "If the truth be told, poor Harry was suffering from delusions of grandeur. Like, he told me that fat ambulance chaser was tied in some-how with the FBI, can you believe it? Two clowns sitting on the motel porch—that's how I saw 'em. Two clowns just blow-ing smoke at each other and boozing the afternoon away."

Spider was sealing up the box now and then folding it neatly in half. "Still, I could tell those two *did* go back a few years together. They were always talking about the glory days they'd had in Washington, a decade ago. That part was real enough, I guess." He gave the stringer a long, thoughtful look. "Anyhow, I imagine this guy Fishpaw would be your best bet, if you want the nitty-gritty on what made Harry tick. Accord-ing to Harry, the lawyer hired him now and then as an investi-gator for his criminal cases—so the two of them were more than just friends."

"Okay, sounds like a good lead." Moon scribbled. "You say Fishpaw used to come to the motel for regular gab sessions with Zalenka?"

"That's right." Spider yawned, then began to scratch at the slack gray flesh beneath his chin. "They'd sit on Harry's front stoop and drink Rolling Rock, while they told each other lies about how important they were. Or they'd discuss the shit Harry was digging up as Fishpaw's investigator—during his brief periods of sobriety, that is.

"As a matter of fact, Fishpaw dropped by Number Six the night before Harry disappeared."

"Did he? And when was that?"

"Aw… I guess it was five, maybe six days ago."

"Okay, so what happened during that last visit?"

"The usual, that's all. Lots of boozing and lots of bullshit. They sat out front of Number Six for a couple of hours. I re-member it because I noticed Fishpaw was drinking from a bot-tle of Bombay gin. Expensive stuff, for a change. He put most of it away, too. I had my door cracked open, and whenever they yelled at each other—which was often—I could hear 'em loud and clear. Zalenka kept barking: 'I've got the evidence, Mel, and maybe it's time to go public with it!'

"And Fishpaw kept on snapping back at him: 'You don't know what you're fooling with, Harry—leave it alone.'

"You know how them lawyers talk."

"I do."

Spider groaned and then rose to his feet. "You want more details, go see Fishpaw. He's over near Salisbury. Law office in Pocomoke City. Easy to find."

"Thanks a lot, Mr. Yarnell. I'll get right on it."

Spider lifted the *Taco Bell* bag carefully, then hook-shot it toward the green plastic trash can in the corner. "Nothing but net!" He stood up. "Okay, you got what you wanted, Mr. *People*. Now when do I get what *I* want? How soon will I show up in the magazine? I want my little honey to see me on that cover. She thinks I'm just another sorry redneck with nothing going for him. Can you believe it?"

Moon was on his feet now. "I'll do the best I can, Spider. The Zalenka story will be on the newsstands next week. Thanks for the help." He leaned over and shook the geezer's hand.

"Fine and dandy," said the old man in the baseball cap. "Fine and dandy!" Then he looked the stringer in the eye. "If I was you, I *would* take a run over to Pocomoke City. I'd talk to Fishpaw. Might be more to this whole thing than meets the eye."

"You bet," said Moon. "I will do that. And I thank you."

"Aren't you going to take my picture?"

"No, I don't take the pictures," said the stringer. "I just collect the words. Another poor devil will be along in a while to take your photo."

Spider nodded. He seemed happy with the arrangement. "Okay, Jim dandy," he said with a smirk. "I'll put a shirt on when he gets here."

5. TEN SOLID MINUTES
OF ASS-RIP

He called Yang immediately. And paid for it.

"Where the fuck have you been, Moon? And where is *Zalenkadrown*? You vanished from the radar screen, dodo."

He backpedaled. "I'm making my rounds, Yang."

"Your rounds? As in, 'Let's have another round?' Are you drunk, you useless turkey-dick?"

"Of course not. I'm working on the file. *Zalenkadrown.* Still assembling the prose."

She snorted. "We don't pay you for prose, bozo. We pay for *information*. Just type the shit out. And hurry. What've you got so far?"

"Well, for starters... Zalenka was a drunk."

A silence. Then an explosion. "No shit, Sherlock! They've only been making that point on CNN for the past 36 hours or so. Please tell me you have something more than that for me."

"That's pretty much it, so far."

"You're shitting me! What have you been doing, Moon? Sitting in a tavern, or pulling your pud?"

"Neither. I'm busting ass, Yang. Really. I interviewed this old guy at The Evening Breeze Motel... Spider."

"Spider? That's his name? Are you for real?"

"He says Zalenka was sitting on some information about a scandal of some kind—a big scandal inside the U.S. Government."

"Are you making this shit up or what?"

"No. This is serious, Yang. The guy's real name is George Yarnell. Spider's just his nickname. I found him in Cabin Nine. He was eating *Taco Bell*. Told me he'd known Zalenka like a brother. Said the poor bastard was drinking himself to death. He's convinced Zalenka was on the road to becoming a wet brain. Boozing compulsively, totally out of control... an addictive personality, that kind of stuff."

"I do know the type," said Yang. "You just described the typical *People* stringer."

"Spider says Zalenka's wife dumped him a while back. His kids haven't spoken to him in years. The poor bastard was falling apart."

"Aren't we all? How was he paying the rent?"

"Spider says he'd been hanging out with a shyster criminal lawyer of some kind over on Maryland's Eastern Shore. Pocomoke City, about 80 miles east of here. A guy named Fishpaw. A great big fat guy. Fishpaw hired Zalenka occasionally as an investigator, so he could earn a few bucks. Listen, I'm all over it, Yang; don't worry about a thing."

"You're all over *what*, Moon? So far, I don't hear anything promising, and I don't hear anything solid. The truth is, we're four days from deadline, and you don't have jack-shit." She paused for a moment and he could hear the wheels turning. "Okay, maybe we can use some of the stuff about the boozing and gambling. And the wife—she broke his heart, right?"

"If you say so."

"Good. He's heartbroken because the wife dumped him, and his family's in tatters... and so he jumps off his sailboat wearing all these diving weights. The sorrow and the pity. The agony and the ecstasy. Mr. Smith goes to Washington and meets the Widow-Maker! The tragic demise of a U.S. Congressman!"

"Whatever you say, Yang."

"Did you get any decent quotes from this... this Spider guy?"

"You bet."

"Such as?"

Moon squinted through the glare, struggled to read the words in his frayed notebook. "Well, let's see... how about: 'Harry was a human train wreck, mister, and I guess he derailed right here at the Last Resort Motel. I'm talking about burning boxcars and twisted metal, *compadre*. There's a saying at AA: One drink's too many, and a thousand drinks ain't enough!' Did you ever hear that saying, Yang?"

Yang groaned. "That's nothing more than the usual AA horseshit. But I do like the part about the train wreck. I assume you made that up? Does Spider mind if you invent some dialogue for him?"

"Wait a minute—I don't make up quotes, Yang. He really said that. Honest."

"Hey, I don't give a damn if you made it up, cowboy—as long as the source doesn't challenge the quote later. I hope he gave you a free hand to invent any shit you want for the story. Do we have some poetic license here, or what?"

"Well, pretty much... as long as we quote him by name. I think we can do whatever we want, for the most part. He's desperate to get into the magazine."

"Aren't they all? Did you find Zalenka's squeeze yet?"

"How's that?"

"Did you find the dead guy's squeeze? Come on, get with it: Who was he fucking at the end? I don't have all day here."

"Jesus, Yang. I'm just getting started."

"You were supposed to get started last night, bozo-reeno."

"I'm doing my best."

"I don't want your best; I want a great fucking story. Find his girlfriend, sleuth."

"I don't think he had one."

"Oh, bullshit. *Everybody* has a girlfriend. Use your wits. Find the divorced wife. Find the squeeze. Find his mother, for Chrissakes. Find me a woman, Moon, *any* woman. Make one up if you have to. Goddamit, get me a woman who will weep for the death of Harry Zalenka, and find her fast! Do you understand?"

"I do."

"Our readers want to feel the pain of the woman he left behind. That's the key to our success at *People*. It's our *raison d'être*. It's why we're the most-read magazine on the planet. Make the wife cry over the loss of her hubby—or make the mother blubber over the death of her little boy. It's all the same to our readers. And it never fails. Make a woman cry, and our millions of readers will cry along with her—even as they shell out their $2.79 at the supermarket checkout counter."

"I hear you."

"No, you don't. That's the whole problem here. What's wrong with you, Moon?"

"Wrong with me? Why, nothing! Nothing at all."

"Bullshit. Tell Momma Yang. What is the fucking *problem*, Moon? Don't you like your job?"

"I do."

"I don't believe you."

"You know I love *People* magazine, Yang."

She sighed. "Get on your horse, Moon. And use the whip. Get me some romance. Get me some heartbreak. Get me some *tears*, you sonofabitch. Find Momma Zalenka and make her weep for her son!"

"Yes, ma'am. Will do."

"I want a file by six o'clock, or the vultures will be feeding on your spleen."

6. WILD MOUSE

Keera would be home from softball practice by now.

He dialed the number for her mother's place in suburban Towson.

"Keera, it's your pappy."

"Hi, Dad. I'm watching *The Brady Bunch*. Where are you?" Keera always wanted to know where he was.

"I'm over on the Eastern Shore, honey. Halfway to your favorite place on earth."

She brightened. "Ocean City?"

"You bet, babe."

"They've got a brand-new roller coaster this year. A monster!"

"Do they now?"

"Yup. The Wild Mouse. I read about it in the *Sun*. A couple of eighth-graders fainted."

"You're kidding."

"Heck, no. The paper said two kids stepped off the Wild Mouse at the end of the ride and fainted dead away. Couldn't take it. They fell flat on the boardwalk!"

He was trying to picture it. Fainting teenagers! "Keera, I think we're gonna have to take a ride."

"No, we *won't*."

"Come on, where's your nerve?"

She sent up a tiny scream. "*Daaaaa*-dd! Do you know how *high* that thing is?"

"No, I don't." Moon always liked it when his daughter gave him facts and figures.

"It's 285 feet, straight up. That's one and a half football fields high! Can you imagine?"

"Pretty hairy, hon. Do they give you a parachute?"

"Stop it, Dad. Why are you on the Shore?"

"A story."

"*People*?"

"That's it. A political story. The tragic death of a United States Congressman. I'm sure it would bore you silly."

"I like to read the magazine when you're in it, Dad."

"I'm glad to hear that, sweetheart—because you're my favorite reader. Hey, how's your mom's boyfriend treating you today?"

"Oh... *him*. Everything's fine. Just peachy—provided we don't talk. And we don't. Do you care if I cuss?"

"Go right ahead, Wild Thing."

"He's a total shitface."

Moon shook his head. "Come on, Keera. Be nice to him. Don't break your momma's heart."

"It's not fair, Dad. What he's doing to her."

"That's not your business, butternut. Leave it alone. Keep a low profile. Besides, whoever told you life was going to be fair?"

She was silent for a few seconds, and he could feel her vexation—her ancient, hovering woe—seeping into his undefended ear. He didn't like that. He never wanted to think of her as wounded. "Hey, Keera, I better get back to work. But I'm really looking forward to tomorrow afternoon—*Jurassic Park*!"

"Same here, Dad. Can't wait!"

"I'll pick you up at four o'clock, same as every Tuesday, okay?"

"You bet!"

"And Keera?"

"Yeah, Dad?"

"I love you big time."

"Love you, too."

"Bye, now." He clicked the phone off and sat holding it for a few seconds. It was nearly three o'clock by now; the shadows were beginning to lengthen along the gravel driveway of The Evening Breeze. He put the Chevy into gear, then drifted onto eastbound Route 50. He was smiling a little.

Keera always made him smile.

7. ALMOST FAMILY!

Seven p.m, Monday. It was raining again. The stringer eased the Sprint into a parking space and cut the ignition. Ten feet above his head, a brightly colored billboard announced that the folks who lived in this olive-drab high-rise nursing home were savoring their Golden Years to the fullest.

Almost Family! Where Senior Citizens Thrive!

"My God," Moon told the empty car. "The horror!" He sat staring at the stark cinderblock walls, at the rusted tin gutters dripping in the steady rain. Thriving, were they? Living the good life on Golden Pond? What was it Diane Arbus had said, right before the end? *To live in our culture is to live in a state of permanent torture.* She'd have felt right at home at *Almost Family!*

No, the Mooner did not appreciate this assignment. He didn't want to share Golden Memories with these dying seniors. He didn't want to smell their dried urine, or watch them drool on their bibs, either. He knew he would *not* enjoy the shrieking and the babbling on the Alzheimer's Ward. Diaper-changing time! But Moon was a *People* stringer, and he would do his job. "Find Momma Zalenka," Yang had said, "and make her weep for her dead son!"

But it wouldn't be easy. Momma Z lived on the fourth floor of *Almost Family!*—according to the latest update from AP— and the nursing home had declared her totally off-limits to the news media. No interviews, period.

Moon's loathsome task: Find a way to get past security and then worm a couple of hard-hitting sound bites from the old lady.

Groaning inwardly, he climbed out of the car and limped toward the front of the high-rise. A TV crew—*News at Eleven!*—had just been given the boot, apparently. Heads down and obviously disgusted, they trudged toward him... with the cameraman bent almost double beneath his heavy equipment and the reporter still wearing his pancake makeup and bright TV lipstick. Moon recognized Buzz Harundale, *News At Eleven's* veteran night-side reporter and a minor Baltimore celebrity.

"Yo, Buzz!" The stringer vibrated with ersatz chumminess. "What's happening in there, my man?"

"Total frustration, that's what." Buzz was rubbing his left eye, where a fragment of TV-mascara had become lodged. "They just kicked our asses out of the lobby, Moon. The place is crawling with security guards. I wouldn't even bother, if I were you."

"Damn Sam," said Moon. "Gave you the boot, did they? Nice try, though. Has anybody gotten to her yet?"

The newscaster moaned. "Not on your life, pal. They told us she's on four, but nobody's allowed up there. No media, anyway. Dementia is what I heard. I talked to a couple of residents in the lobby—they said she's completely senile. Babbles all this crazy shit night and day." He grimaced as he dug at his inflamed eye. "No press admitted—and they've got three different rent-a-cops bird-dogging the lobby, stopping anybody who tries to board an elevator or take the stairs."

He sighed and shook his head. "They won't let anybody onto the floors without a nursing-home I.D. or a signed guest-card from a resident, so we're shit out of luck."

Moon nodded. "I see. Too bad. Well, thanks, Buzz."

He waved once, then he turned around in his tracks and drifted slowly back toward the car. But he didn't get in. Instead, he popped open the trunk and removed a white lab coat. A quick look around told him the coast was clear. Moving fast, he slipped into the coat and then adjusted the hand-lettered name-tag pinned to its front pocket: *Dr. T.J. Moon/AF/PhilaHQ.* Perfect!

Next he grabbed the plastic clipboard he'd stashed in the trunk and slammed the door shut. So far, so good. Ambling slowly along, resisting the urge to hurry, he wandered around one side of the high-rise and approached the loading docks behind it. As he'd expected, the back of the complex was crowded with service vehicles and delivery trucks: *Hamrick's Produce, Ajax Plumbing, Boston Chicken.* But the drivers were nowhere in sight—apparently, this was their dinner hour.

Moving more swiftly now, Moon eased between two trucks... then hopped quickly onto a loading platform. Clipboard at the ready, he strode purposefully toward the nearest door. It was open, and he soon found himself hustling through a dimly lit storeroom where crates of canned fruit juice were stacked floor to ceiling. He could hear water running somewhere. He stepped gingerly across the wet red tiles... then froze. A sleepy-looking factotum in a white paper hat marked *Almost Family!* stood blocking his path. *Uh-oh.*

"Can I help you, doctor?"

Moon's brain raced. Fortunately, his years as a stringer had taught him that the best way to answer questions about your identity is simply to re-phrase them and fire them back at the interrogator.

"Is there some way I can help *you*, son?" Moon pointed at his name tag. Then, as the clerk hesitated: "I'm Dr. T.J. Moon from Philadelphia HQ, as you can see."

"Yes, sir," said the clerk. "I see that."

"I'm from Pharmaceutical Inventory. The Pill People. Did you get my call?"

"Your call, sir?" The man in the paper hat eyed him uncertainly.

"That's correct. I called earlier. The inventory? For Pharmaceutical? You know about the inventory by Philadelphia HQ?"

The clerk gaped at him. "I didn't... I never..."

"Look here," snapped Dr. Moon. "Do you or *don't* you know about the Inventory Audit by Philadelphia HQ??" When the factotum hesitated again, mouth hanging open, Moon took command. "Tell you what," he said. "You just hang on here. Go about your business, and I'll get back to you in a few minutes."

Without hesitating, he pushed past the staring clerk, strode over to the nearest door and pushed it open. The dim interior was crammed with mops and buckets.

"Ah... that's the broom closet, sir."

Moon nodded brusquely. "Thank you for your guidance, young man." He turned, cleared his throat, and then spotted a red arrow marked: *Service Elevator*. Eyes narrowed, heart pounding, he walked in the direction suggested by the arrow. At any moment, he expected to hear the warehouse worker's shouted command: "Hold it, mister—I need to see some I.D.!'" But the command never came.

Breathing more easily now, he scuttled down a dank corridor and eased into an open elevator: *All Floors*. He took the metal box up to four and stepped off into a noisy hallway. The walls were painted chocolate-brown and he sniffed a faint tang of human urine. He began moving from room to room, pausing only to read the scrawled last names on the index cards pinned to the door frames.

Bingo! He was halfway down the hallway when he came upon the name: *Zalenka, Doris D*. He poked his head a little way into the room. A tiny, white-haired woman with an enormous wart over one eye sat on a bed. She wore a blue gown patterned with dime-sized bluebells. The old woman held a yellow plastic hairbrush in one hand and a stuffed toy lion in the other. He watched her slowly brushing the animal's mane.

"Good evening," said the stringer. He glided smoothly toward the bed. "Hello, there! My name is Tommy Moon. I assume you're Mrs. Zalenka?"

She stopped brushing. "Depends on who wants to know."

"*People* magazine wants to know," said the stringer. "The editors asked me to convey their deepest regrets about your son. All of us feel your pain, at *People*; we're suffering right along with you."

(This was the standard *People* approach, of course, when interviewing grieving relatives of the dead.)

"My name's Doris," said the woman on the bed. She spoke in a childish singsong. "I drew a yellow parrot downstairs in the Art Room. And I don't *have* no pain, mister, no real pain at all. The doc gave me a brace for my hip, but sometimes I use a cane."

Moon stared at her. "You drew a parrot?"

She rocked with childish laughter. "*Big* old parrot, bright yellow. Drew him with my Crayola!"

Moon considered this answer. Dementia? All at once, he realized that the old lady might not even know about the drowning. Not good. Goddamit... he had to get those sound bites!

"Mrs. Zalenka, I was actually referring to your son, when I mentioned your pain. Poor Harry, I mean. His was a terrible tragedy, and we all share your deep sorrow."

"Harry?" Doris looked up from her brushing. "Hoo-boy! I told that little peckerwood he better keep out of trouble, or I'll kick his ass into the next county. That little sonofabitch and his antics... the last time he got locked up for drunk and disorderly, he nearly broke his momma's heart."

"The last time?"

She snuffled wetly and kept brushing the mane. "You bet. He got his ass thrown in the clink twice during senior year for fighting the cops. What an a-hole! I'll always love him, of course—he's my boy, after all. But that don't mean Harry ain't an a-hole!"

Moon blinked at her. "Mrs. Zalenka... are you with me here? Have you been told that your son fell into the Chesapeake Bay?"

Doris giggled, then waved the hairbrush at him. "That little shitbird—if he fell in, he better dry off, or he'll wind up with pneumonia to beat the band!"

The stringer took a deep breath. It was now or never. "Mrs. Zalenka, your son Harry is dead. He drowned in the Bay. He's gone. I'm very sorry. Believe me, we share your pain, at *People*. But he's gone. How do you feel about that?" (It was the most important single question in all of contemporary journalism, and as a *People* stringer, Moon was required to ask it several times a week: *How do you feel about the tragic death of your loved one?*)

But Mrs. Zalenka didn't seem fazed by the query.

She was grinning at him. "Mister, you don't know jackshit!" Once again, she waggled the hairbrush at him. "My little peckerwood ain't dead. How could he be dead? He's been living in my basement the last few years—with all his furniture and all his books! He lives in my house at Tower Oaks, way down there in the basement. He's my boy, my little Harry!"

Moon felt his pulse speeding up as he ignored the gibberish and wrote only the sound bites he'd just been hearing into his notebook. They were pure gold!

Bite # 1: "I'll always love him... he's my boy!"

Bite #2: "How could he be dead?

Bite #3: "He's my boy, my little Harry!"

Moon had himself a winner. By stringing these three bites together—while completely ignoring the rest of Mrs. Zalenka's commentary—he could easily assemble the weepy tearjerker that Yang required. *(Congressman's Mother Grieves Dead Son: Heartbreak in Baltimore—A People Exclusive!)*

He scribbled. He watched her comb the lion's mane, and he scribbled some more. But then a shadow fell over the bed. The shadow had been thrown by a very tall nurse with iron-gray hair. Her mouth seemed cold, stern.

"Excuse me, sir. Why are you in this room?"

"Me? I'm Dr. T.J. Moon from Philadelphia *Almost Family!* We're doing a pharmaceutical audit and I'm making my rounds." He pointed to the I.D. tag on his white lab coat.

She glared at him. "I beg your pardon, sir. I wasn't informed about an audit, or about a visit from Philadelphia. And rounds are at ten a.m., not seven in the evening. If you're a visiting physician, you need to check in with Medical Registration. Second floor. This room is off-limits. Please follow me."

Moon did so—and grilled her as best he could, while they walked toward the elevators. "Nurse, I can't believe no one has informed Mrs. Zalenka about her son's accidental death."

The nurse glared even harder. "Dr. Moon, that patient is 86 years old, and she has advanced Alzheimer's. She can't remember anything she's heard for more than two minutes. And I believe she *has* been told of her son's tragic passing."

"I see."

The nurse was eagle-eyeing his name-tag. Then suddenly, out of the blue: "With all due respect, sir—I think we need to stop by the nurses' station and verify your I.D. Are you from corporate? Is this a public relations thing, or what?"

Moon's smile had frozen on his face. "Me? I'm from Philadelphia HQ. I'm with the *Almost Family!* Pharmaceutical Audit."

He tried to give her a reassuring smile, but she refused to meet his eye. She was onto him—no question about it! But then he got a stroke of good luck—they were passing the same service elevator on which he'd arrived. Moving quickly, Moon hopped into the tiny car and hit the CLOSE button. The doors began to rumble shut. The nurse's eyes grew huge as she realized the worst: The intruder was taking flight! Now she was shouting: "Wait a minute—hold it! Stop that elevator this minute!"

As the car began its clattering descent, he could hear her sneakered feet already pounding down the hall. She was running for the rent-a-cops!

But it was no contest.

Moon was safely back in the Sprint—scribbled sound-bites at the ready—at least 30 seconds before her club-carrying *police* hit the *Almost Family!* parking lot.

Chortling happily, he watched them grow smaller and smaller in his rear-view mirror, as the Chevy sped down Harford Road and into the rainy evening.

8. THE GRIEVING DIVORCEE:
3 BITES

Sometimes, you just plain get lucky. Locating the former Mrs. Harry Zalenka turned out to be as simple as flipping through an old *Congressional Yearbook* and reading the "Thumbnail Sketch" of the Democratic congressman from Salisbury, the largest city on Maryland's Eastern Shore. *Family: Mr. Zalenka married the former Meredith Anne Staples of Chesapeake City, Md., in 1972, but the marriage ended in divorce in 1990....*

Moon thought about it. What would a woman named "Meredith Anne Staples" do after her marriage of 19 years ended in divorce?

She'd head home, that's what. She'd want to return to the tranquil, small-town world she'd known before meeting her hard-drinking congressman.

Bingo: C&P Telephone had her listed as "M. Staples" in Chesapeake City, and when Moon dialed the number, she answered on the second ring.

"Hello?" A female voice, middle-aged.

"Good evening," said the stringer. "Are you Ms. Staples?"

A pause. He could hear her thinking on the other end of the line. How many reporters had already called her in search of the dirty details about her marriage to Harry Zalenka? "Would you identify yourself, please?" The voice was cold and clipped.

Moon's vocal tone deepened into Funeral Director-mode. "Ms. Staples, first of all, I want you to know how sorry we are for your trouble."

Another long pause. "Who is 'we,' please? You better identify yourself, before I hang up."

"I'm Tommy Moon," he said smoothly, "and my editors at *People* have asked me to convey their deepest regards. They share your pain, ma'am, they really do."

"The editors at *where*?" Her voice bristled with permafrost.

"We all know how much your loss hurts, ma'am. We're all feeling the devastation, even as you must be."

"What devastation? Who the hell *is* this? Did you say *People* magazine?"

"Yes, I did. And I have only a single question for you, Ms. Staples: How did you feel when you learned that your former husband had drowned in the Chesapeake Bay?"

She hesitated for at least five seconds. (Moon could never understand why people in this situation didn't just hang up. But they never did. They simply couldn't resist the temptation to blast the reporter who'd dared to ask about the death of their loved one. Because they were suffering, they felt they had a license to rip the reporter's head off, and they always attacked viciously, without remorse.)

"You bastard!" M. Staples growled, right on cue. "Can I ask *you* a question, you despicable sonofabitch?"

Moon braced for the assault. "Ma'am, I'm *sorry*, I truly am. I can tell you're upset." His voice quivered with feigned empathy, feigned self-reproach. "I deeply regret having to ask you about all of this. But please go ahead."

She snorted with indignation. "Mr. Moon: How does it *feel*... to make your living as a magazine vampire?"

"Ms. Staples, please forgive me," he actually moaned. "The truth is, I *hate* having to call you like this. But we have a job to do, in the news media –"

"Bullshit! Don't hand me that crap!" She was shouting now, and enjoying herself fully. "You loathsome parasite! You total scumbag! Did it even once occur to you—before you dialed this number—that I might be grieving for the man I was married to for 18 years? You bloodsuckers in the news media… I didn't sleep a wink last night, and every time I turn on the TV, I'm looking at my wedding photo all over CNN!

"This whole thing has been pure torture, and now *you* show up, determined to make it even worse. You vicious prick, I hope this happens to *you* someday!"

Moon winced as she slammed the phone down.

But then he let loose with a whoop of triumphant laughter. *Yeah! Nailed her!* Nailed her *cold!* Talk about scoring some juicy sound-bites!

Bite No. 1: Ms. Staples described herself as "*…grieving for the man I was married to for18 years.*"

Bite No. 2: Ms. Staples has been suffering terribly since the drowning: "*I didn't sleep a wink last night, and every time I turn on the TV, I'm looking at my wedding photo all over CNN.*"

Bite No. 3: Look how much she misses her former husband. "*This whole thing has been pure torture!*"

Pure gold. By combining these bites with the bites from Momma Zalenka and then tossing in some reporting details he'd stolen from the Baltimore *Sun* and the Washington *Post*, Moon could easily crank out the tearjerker Stringer File Yang Yang was demanding: *The Heart-Breaking Saga of the Women Harry Left Behind!*

9. FIRST STRINGER FILE

***People* Stringer File #1477**
Date: *Monday, Aug. 14, 1995, 10 p.m.*
To: *YANG YANG, National Stringer Desk*
From: *T. MOON, Baltimore*
Subject: *Zalenkadrown, 1st file*

KENT ISLAND, MD.—His tragic death by drowning broke their hearts.

When 86-year-old Doris Zalenka learned that the body of her son—former U.S. Congressman Harry J. Zalenka (Democrat, Maryland, 1981-83)—had been found on the shores of the Chesapeake Bay on Sunday, she wept bitterly.

"How could he be dead?" Doris Zalenka wailed from her nursing home bed in Baltimore, as she succumbed to her overwhelming grief. "I'll always love him. He's my boy! My little Harry!"

Like Doris Zalenka, the dead congressman's former wife—Meredith Anne Staples, 53—seemed stunned by the knowledge that the 57-year-old Zalenka was gone from her life forever.

In an exclusive *People* interview, Staples said she was ". . . grieving for the man I was married to for 18 years. I didn't sleep a wink last night, and every time I turn on the TV, I'm looking at our wedding photo all over CNN!"

Describing the twists and turns her pain-wracked life has taken since Zalenka's body washed up beneath the Catch O' The Day Fishing Pier yesterday, Staples cried out in anguish: "This whole thing has been pure torture!"

Nobody knows exactly what happened to the former congressman, who represented Maryland's sparsely populated Eastern Shore region for a single term more than a decade ago.

The discovery of Zalenka's badly decomposed body, which had reportedly been in the water for several days, has triggered a number of troubling questions, including these:

• Did Zalenka fall off his 27-foot sloop, the *Razzmatazz*? According to the U.S.Coast Guard, Zalenka checked the sailboat out of its rented mooring slip at Turkey Point on the Choptank River near Easton, Maryland, five days before his body washed ashore on nearby Kent Island. So far, there has been no sign of the missing sloop.

• Why was Zalenka wearing a scuba-diving belt containing 40 pounds of lead weights when his body drifted ashore?

• Why was the congressman living in a rundown motel in the rural enclave of Trappe, Md. (population: 1,146) during the three months before he suddenly vanished?

• How long had Zalenka been dead when his heavily weighted body surfaced beneath the fishing pier on Kent Island?

According to reports from the Maryland State Police, Zalenka's body will be autopsied tomorrow (Associated Press), as investigators attempt to learn more about the circumstances surrounding his death. Meanwhile, Medical Examiner Harold Pangborn, M.D., has refused to speculate about the case, while telling reporters: "We don't talk about ongoing investigations, and I haven't seen the body yet—so don't waste your breath asking me questions I can't answer." (Reuters)

At this point (Monday evening, 7 p.m.), only one thing seems clear: Harry Zalenka was down and out at the end of his life. According to several people who knew him in his final days, he'd been living for several months at the decaying Evening Breeze Motel in Trappe, a tiny Maryland fishing and crabbing community located about 20 miles east of Kent Island.

"I can tell you for a fact that Harry Zalenka was a deeply, deeply troubled man," said George ("Spider") Yarnell, an elderly retiree who lives in Unit No. Nine of The Evening Breeze. "Poor Harry was a drunk, that's all. It's that simple. He sat over there in Number Six, drinking malt liquor and listening to Roy Orbison tapes all day. Harry must've listened to *Only the Lonely* ten thousand times. He was a human train wreck, and I guess he derailed right here at the Last Resort Motel. I'm talking about burning boxcars and twisted metal—total human wreckage, if you catch my drift? His wife dumped him five or six years ago and his grownup kids wanted no part of him, either.

"There's a saying in AA: 'One drink is too many, and a thousand drinks ain't enough.' I begged Harry to attend AA meetings with me, but he wouldn't listen."

File Summary: Thirty-six hours after the discovery of Harry Zalenka's body, two suffering women—the two women Harry had loved most in the world, his mother and his former spouse—are now grieving terribly for the former lawmaker.

Sitting on her bed in Room 411 of the *Almost Family!* nursing home in Baltimore, Doris Zalenka clutched a furry toy lion that had once belonged to her son.

"How could he be dead?" she asked again and again, as she hugged the stuffed animal to her heaving breast.

"My little Harry!"

END MOON STRINGER FILE #1477

Monday, 8/14/95

10. YET ANOTHER
DEVASTATING ASS-RIP

Twenty minutes after the stringer wired the file to New York, his Nokia began to chatter.

"Hello, Yang."

"What is this shit, Moon?"

Moon blinked. He made fists of his hands. "Hey, it's what you asked for, isn't it? Heartbreak? Two grieving women? His momma weeps for him! She loved her little boy! She can't believe he's dead! You fucking slave driver—isn't that precisely what you *asked* for?"

Yang made a sniggering sound on the other end. "I love it when you insult me, Moon. Why? Because it's the only time you ever tell me the truth. Okay, so you've made a small start here. You've given me some weepy shit. Fine. But where's the juicy political drama? Where's the detective work? The inside scoop? Our readers want to know how he died. *Why* he died. Why aren't you talking to the state cops, the Coast Guard, the Medical Examiner?"

"Give me time, Yang. Jesus! I'm working with a very real limitation here—the unfortunate fact that I can only be in one place at a time."

"Bullshit. You know more than you've put into this file. I can smell it. You're hiding something from me—something hot. Why does a former member of the United States Congress end up in the drink? And why is he wrapped in diving weights when he finally surfaces? What the fuck is going *on* here, Moon?"

"Nothing at all," groaned Moon. "Certainly nothing that would interest *People*, anyway. There's no political story here, Yang. The guy was a sad drunk, that's all, and he fell off his boat. Or maybe he went scuba diving and never returned. End of saga.   Close the book. Good night, Irene. You got your weepy sound bites—so call in your writers and tell 'em to start breaking rocks. Tell your 30 million readers about the women Harry left behind, and let's move on."

"Sorry, Moon, no can do. I want the lowdown, shit-for-brains. I want to know what happened on that boat. Did he drown on his own, or did he require assistance?"

"I can't help you there, Yang. All I've got are a couple of rumors. Some gossip, nothing more."

"Gossip? We *live* on gossip at *People*. Let me hear it, shit-bird."

Moon hesitated. *I need major vodka, and soon.* "There isn't much, Yang. Barely a whisper. Remember Spider, that guy who lives at the motel? Well... he told me Zalenka was always talking about a scandal on Capitol Hill."

"Yeah, so I recall. And I notice you left all that good stuff out of your file. Why? Level with me, turkey."

"It was pure hearsay, Yang. Just some idle speculation from an old redneck."

She snorted. "Hearsay? Who are you, Louie Nizer? *I'm* the one who decides what's hearsay around here. What was Zalenka saying before he died?"

Moon sighed and shook his head. "Well, according to Spider, Zalenka claimed to have some inside dope on a spy scandal that had taken place back around 1980."

"A spy scandal? Now that's more *like* it! Particulars, please?"

"Okay, this is going to sound ridiculous... which is why I didn't put it in the stringer file! But if you must know—Spider said Zalenka claimed to have uncovered a Soviet mole inside the CIA. This was a decade before the Berlin Wall came down, remember, back when the struggle between the U.S. and the Soviet Union was still a matter of life and death. Anyway, he—Zalenka, I mean—was convinced that the CIA mole had never been caught… that he was still at work and still feeding information to the Russians."

Yang sent up a loud guffaw. "Good boy! A treacherous mole inside the CIA? I dig it! What kind of information was he peddling?"

"I don't know, Yang. Spider was pretty vague. Satellite stuff, I think he said. You know… spy-in-the-sky-type info. He mentioned a surveillance system of some kind.   Big Bird? Yeah, that's it. Big Bird. According to Spider, Zalenka had dug up some evidence showing how the mole had leaked the engineering on Big Bird to the Russkies. And then right before he vanished, just a few days ago, the congressman—*former* congressman, I mean—had been threatening to go public with his info.

"But he never got the chance, apparently."

"Wait a minute, nerd-o! Are you telling me you heard scuttlebutt linking Zalenka to a Russian mole, and you didn't put that shit in your file? You had evidence of possible *espionage*, and you kept it to yourself?"

Moon was shaking his head. "Come on, Yang. That stuff was totally dubious. For chrissakes, the source for all of it was an old hillbilly in a baseball cap!"

"Who cares where it came from? And who cares if it's true? It's *interesting*, no-nuts, and it's lots of fun. How many times have I told you: Whatever you do, never, ever let facts get in the way of a good story? Now tell Momma Yang: does anybody else know about this spy shit?"

"I don't think so. Well… maybe one guy. According to Spider, Zalenka was close pals with a country lawyer over on the Eastern Shore of Maryland. A guy named Fishpaw. Apparently, the two of them went way back. Melvin Fishpaw. A great big fat guy, drank a lot of gin. Spider said he used to drop by the motel every few days… and the two of them would sit on the porch out in front of Number Six, boozing and bullshitting the afternoon away.

"Spider said he used to eavesdrop on the two of them… mainly because he didn't have anything better to do. According to the old gaffer at the motel, Zalenka was forever threatening to tell what he knew. Every time he got tanked up, he'd yell at the lawyer: 'If I go public with this stuff, it'll blow the lid right off Washington.'

"Fishpaw didn't seem impressed, however. Whenever Harry mouthed off about the mole, Harry would tell him to shut his mouth before somebody shut it for him."

Yang made a low, whistling sound somewhere deep in her sinuses. "Holy rat shit. This could be big, Mooner. Are you telling me Zalenka was sitting on a major spy scandal… and threatening to spill the beans… and then somebody whacked him?"

Moon groaned. "You're speculating, Yang. You're over the line. You're hanging way out there in the ozone layer!"

"Good for me, Moon. Why don't you join me there? Why don't you *work* this story, you dickless wonder? Tell me: Are you too goddam lazy—or simply too goddam chickenshit—to uncover this Russian mole Zalenka knew about?"

"Holy moly, Yang, you're making tremendous leaps here. There's no evidence for a mole yet, none whatsoever. All we have is what Spider told us. He said Zalenka met with the lawyer the night before he drowned, and the two of them argued at length about Big Bird. But how reliable is that shit, really? I mean, think it through. According to Spider, Fishpaw's nothing more than a rinky-dink ambo-chaser with a fleabag law practice over in Pocomoke City."

Now Yang cut loose with a whoop of laughter. "Pocomoke City? Are you kidding me? What a name! It's wonderful. It's priceless. Our readers will love it, Moon."

"Yang… this whole thing… it's pure speculation!"

"Find the fat lawyer in Pocomoke City, Moon."

Backpedaling desperately now, the panicked stringer fought to duck what he knew would be an arduous assignment. "Yang, can't you see that we're wasting our time here? We're chasing idle gossip from some dried-up old turkey-neck in a falling-down motel. The Evening Breeze… for shit's sake, even the *locale* sounds ridiculous. Let's move on. Let's call in the writers and break some rocks. Really, I need to get back to chasing Frank Sinatra!"

There was a long pause, while the wheels turned in Yang's close-cropped head. When she finally spoke, her voice was colder than snow-lashed tundra. "I want you to find Fishpaw's fat ass," she snapped at the stringer, "and I want you to find it *pronto*. Grill him within an inch of his life, do you hear me? And do the same with the Maryland state cop who was first on the scene. According to Reuters, he was a patrolman named Mazzoni… here, I've got it right here. Sergeant Al Mazzoni. He's stationed at the Baltimore Inner Harbor, but he happened to be patrolling the area around Kent Island when the first calls about Zalenka's body came in. He's at the Harbor Barracks, at 2450 South Broadway. It's right near the city waterfront, apparently. Find him and get every detail you can on exactly what happened when he found the body. How did the corpse *look*? What did he see? Think you can handle that?"

"I can," lied Moon. "I will, Yang."

"I hope so," she replied, "for the sake of your job security. Find out everything you can about the body. Then you better talk to the Maryland Medical Examiner. What's his name?"

"Pangborn. Dr. Harold Pangborn."

"As soon as he's completed the autopsy, put a full-court press on him. Hound him until he screams. Make him talk, Moon! Find out if he spotted any wound marks on the body. Were there any signs of struggle? Does he think it was a suicide, or does he think it was a murder. An accident? What? Does anybody know?"

"Yes, ma'am. I'm all over it."

"The fuck you are, you useless sheep turd. Get moving, and get moving *now*. Oh, and by the way… Tolliver tried to fire you again this morning, but I managed to stay his hand."

"You are too kind." Moon sighed deeply. "I'll do it, Yang—but I don't understand why you keep raising the bar on me. You told me to get you some sound-bites from the grieving womenfolk, and I gave 'em to you. I delivered! Why can't you just run the bites and leave me alone?"

But Yang ignored this. "Zero in on Melvin Fishpaw, Moon. Find out what he knows and do it ASAP. File some great shit by Wednesday afternoon, or you will taste the cold steel."

"Jesus. What do you *want*, Yang?"

She laughed. It was an ugly, predatory sound. "Don't you get it, doofus? I want it *all*. I want *every*thing! Now get your butt in gear. Work harder. Move faster. Push every lead. We've only got 96 hours before we have to close the next edition of *People* magazine!"

Click.

TUESDAY

1. LUNCH WITH SGT. MAZZONI

Sergeant Al Mazzoni ate lunch every day at the Polock Johnny's Coney Island on Baltimore's Inner Harbor... and it was there that Moon finally caught up with him. Moon had spent the morning making useless phone calls—to the U.S. Coast Guard ("No comment"), to the brass at the Maryland State Police ("No comment"), and to half a dozen current and former members of the U.S. House of Representatives who'd known Zalenka during his brief time on Capitol Hill (half a dozen "No comments").

It was Tuesday now, a little after noon, and the stringer had exactly *zilch* to show for his efforts.

He found Mazzoni sitting at a little tin table near the water's edge. It was a mild blue August afternoon, with a few fluffy white clouds drifting above the giant Eastside Trash Incinerator (aka "The Cancer Works") on the city's smog-layered waterfront.

Mazzoni was eating a hot dog the size of an NFL football as Moon approached his table. The dog was pincered inside a giant slab of greasy bologna that had been drenched with chili, beans, chopped raw onions, melted American cheese and at least half a pint of bright yellow mustard. These locally famous "Coney Island Dogs" were a foot long and dangerously radioactive, but thousands of Balti-morons were addicted to them.

"Sergeant Mazzoni?"

The diner looked up from his unholy feast. "Who are you?" he said.

"I'm Tommy Moon," said the stringer. "I'm a reporter for *People* magazine."

"Why are you interrupting my lunch, and how did you find me?"

Moon answered in reverse order: "They told me you always eat here, over at the State Police Barracks on Broadway. I'm interrupting your lunch in order to interview you."

"Those bastards," said Mazzoni.

"I'm working on a story about Harry Zalenka," said the stringer. He held out his right hand for a shake.

But the irked state cop ignored it. He was a short, stumpy-looking man with wet blue eyes and a brushy, poorly groomed mustache. "I don't comment about ongoing investigations," he growled.

Moon slid onto the rickety chair that faced him. "Why are you sitting down?" said Mazzoni.

"I'm feeling kind of hungry," said Moon. "How are the dogs?"

"Same as they've been for the past fifty years at Polock Johnny's," said Mazzoni. "Go away."

"No offense," said Moon, "but you've got a piece of raw onion caught in your mustache."

The state trooper didn't reach for it, however. "Did you not hear me? I said, hit the trail."

"Just one question and I'm off," said the stringer. "Sergeant Mazzoni, I understand that you were the first law enforcement officer called to the Catch O' The Day Pier after Zalenka's body was discovered floating between the pilings.

"My question is: did you see any wound marks on that body? Anything at all to suggest foul play?"

Mazzoni had been holding one end of the dog near his mouth. But now he lowered it slowly to the paper plate. "That's *two* questions, and I ain't about to answer either one."

"Why not?"

"That's *three* questions, and you're really starting to piss me off."

"Sorry," said Moon. "Trooper Mazzoni, I'm just trying to do my job here. I need to know if you spotted any signs of struggle on Zalenka's body."

The lawman's mouth split open in a decidedly unfriendly grin. "No way, Jose. We don't comment on open investigations, period. I'm sure you know that. So why are you fucking up my hot dog?"

"Did you escort the body to the Medical Examiner's Office?"

Mazzoni sighed. His mournful gaze would have been perfect for your typical Italian opera, for the moment right before the Fat Lady sings her final aria. "I'm not going to comment on where the body went or where it *didn't* go," he growled at Moon. "I will tell you one thing, however."

Moon waited, without breathing.

"If I were you, I'd stay away from this one."

"Beg your pardon?"

"You heard me. If it were me, I'd leave this one alone."

"You would?"

"I would."

"Why?"

Mazzoni made a burbling, chuckling sound somewhere deep in his throat. "Let's just say this one might be a little *different* and leave it at that, okay?" He gave the stringer another long and melancholy look. "Did you say you were with *People*?"

"I did."

"Don't you guys mostly cover... like... movie stars with big tits?"

Moon thought for a moment. "I do think that's a fair assessment," he nodded. "But we also attempt to cover other types of stories now and then. Just for the sake of variety, I mean."

Mazzoni produced another brutally ugly smile. "Okay... but don't say you haven't been warned."

A moment later he was raising the big dog toward his mouth again. "Now beat it... before I snap the cuffs on you and take you in."

Moon did as instructed.

Sixty seconds later, he was back behind the wheel of the Chevy Sprint. Frowning with perplexity, he was talking to himself out loud.

"If it were me, I'd leave this one alone."

He reached down and turned the key in the ignition.

What the hell was going *on* here?

2. WITH KEERA

Tuesday afternoon, 5:30. They were sitting at a back table in the Harford Road *Burger King*. They'd just come from two hours of blood-curdling suspense at the Cinema 8 revival of *Jurassic Park*.

"Okay," said the stringer. "Are you ready for the velociraptor?"

"Stop it, Dad," said 15-year-old Keera. But she was grinning and grinning hard, with the August sunlight flashing along her braces. Blue-eyed, with a few pale freckles scattered across the bridge of her nose. His Keera.

"I'm going to do the velociraptor," said Moon. "Brace yourself."

"Dad, I'm warning you!"

But he had both hands up now, and twisted into attack claws. The claws hovered above their Cheese Whoppers and Cherry Cokes.

"He goes like this...." The stringer wiggled his fingers fast. Then he began to make the deep-in-the-throat *cawing* sound that velociraptors make before they fling themselves upon humans. "*Cawwwww...*" he burbled, while his fingers fluttered and twitched, "*cawww... CAWWW!*" And then he went for her. His claw-hands darted across the table toward her neck!

"DAD!"

She sent up a quick scream of laughter. Just one—but it was enough. At least a dozen *Burger King* diners were now staring at them.

"They think we're crazy, Dad!"

"I don't care what they think," he told her. "There's only one thing I care about right now, Keera."

"What's that, Dad?"

He relaxed his hands. "I'm with you."

3. A SURREAL INTERLUDE
WITH MR. FISHPAW

POCOMOKE CITY: Population 6,329.

After dropping Keera off at her mother's condo in suburban Towson, the stringer drove at breakneck speed back across the Chesapeake Bay Bridge and then east toward the Atlantic. By 9 p.m., he was cruising alongside the swampy, mahogany-hued Pocomoke River. Three miles north of town, he pulled the Sprint onto the parking lot of what Melvin Fishpaw had described on the telephone as "the best little ole crab-pot restaurant on the Eastern Shore, quote-and-*un*quote!"

The Chesapeake House—a sagging, tarpaper-roofed shanty at the water's edge—would never make the pages of *The Architectural Review*. But the African-American chef did astonishing things with the famed Atlantic blue crab, according to Harry Zalenka's former pal... and his broiled rockfish in *fra diavolo* sauce had won three different awards from the big-time gourmet magazines. Inside, the décor was 1957 Key West, with ragged fishing nets hanging from the ceiling, giant conch shells serving as ashtrays and a five-foot barracuda grinning from his brass plate above the gleaming bar.

Moon found the fat man sitting at his own private table beside the kitchen door. Had he requested this privileged location so he could stay close to the food? Fishpaw was drinking dark rum and Fresca and nibbling from a jumbo-sized bucket of popcorn shrimp. The lawyer wore a midnight-blue *Kahala* sports shirt covered with silver parrots. Vast and flowing, the Hawaiian-style garment nearly concealed his immense belly, but not quite. Fishpaw was an Easter Island god—a scowling deity with shoulders the size of burial mounds and two tiny pig-eyes that jerked and swiveled as they followed the action at the bar.

"You the *People* guy?"

"That's me," said the stringer. "Tommy Moon. I guess you'd be Mr. Fishpaw?"

"That would be correct. Sit down, *campesino*, and I'll treat you to a frosty beverage. But I need to tell you something first. May I proceed?"

"Sure," said Moon. He fell into a chair. "Fire away."

"Thank you," said Fishpaw. "My message is a simple one: fuck you!"

Moon looked at him. "I beg your pardon?"

"You heard me. I said 'Fuck you,' and I meant '*Fuck you!*'"

Moon had begun climbing to his feet. His face was a swirly mask of cognitive dissonance.

"Aw, sit back down," growled Fishpaw. "Don't get your balls in an uproar. Everything is fine. What're you drinking?"

"Ah... vodka," said Moon. "With Donald Duck OJ. But before we go there, how about explaining what's going on? You told me on the phone you'd be happy to do this interview, as long as we kept it off the record."

Fishpaw nodded. "That's right, and we *will* do the interview. Calm down, for chrissakes." Now the heavyset attorney lifted a handful of popcorn shrimp toward his giant maw. There were at least 10 of the hapless crustaceans trapped in his palm. Without hesitating, he shoved them into the great cavity in his head. "Okay," he growled again, "I didn't actually mean *you* just now, when I said, 'Fuck you.' All right? It wasn't personal, not at all. I was actually referring to that shit-rag you say you represent. *People*. You guys really fucked me, back in '91. I had a client on a major embezzlement case... front-page stuff. My guy had stolen $5 million from the State of Maryland, and he made it look easy."

The big man stopped talking in order to chew. Moon watched the enormous jaws grinding like boulders against the defenseless shrimp.

"Are you saying you didn't like our coverage of the embezzlement story?"

Fishpaw swallowed, and the entire table shook. "Does the Pope eat *pasta e fagiole* on Saturday night in the Vatican? You made my guy look like fuckin' Benito Mussolini on steroids. Three months after you ripped his balls off, the jury convicted him on every single count. He got 10 years in the slammer, no parole."

The stringer frowned. "Was he guilty?"

"Of course he was guilty. What the fuck difference does *that* make? I was all set to do an open-Sesame—and instead he gets 10 years on the rock pile. And why? How could such a terrible injustice occur? It was simple. It happened because your magazine made him the national poster boy for 'Punishing White-Collar Crime.' For stealing a lousy $5 million. Shit, I know congressmen who take home that much in an average month."

Moon nodded. "I hear you. Mr. Fishpaw, the first thing you need to understand about *People* is, we never let facts get in the way of a good story. It sounds to me like your guy just happened to be in the wrong place at the wrong time."

"You making excuses for those slime-dogs?"

"Not really. Especially since I probably hate them even more than you do."

Fishpaw stopped chewing for a moment. "*Hate* them? But you're a staff reporter for *People*, aren't you?"

"Not really. I'm just a news stringer, Mr. Fishpaw. I'm what they call an 'independent contractor'. I get shit for pay and no benefits. Think of me as a kind of journalistic migrant worker and you'll have it right." Moon shrugged. "But what the hell—everybody has to work somewhere, right? All things considered, I'd rather be doing *haiku* poetry, but there aren't any dollars in it."

Fishpaw grunted, then rotated his gargantuan head. "Mandy? *Mandy!*" He tried to snap his flabby fingers, but they were too soft and no sound emerged. "Mandy... goddamit, get your perfect butt over here!" They watched her drift toward their table—a long-legged strawberry blonde in a maroon tank top and freckles.

"Mandy, please bring this gentleman a double *Stoli* with some... what'd you say you take with it?"

"Donald Duck OJ," said Moon.

The waitress scribbled. "Sure thing, Love Bucket."

"And bring him the popcorn shrimp as well."

"Ten-four," said Mandy. "I'm on it, counselor." She was already walking toward the snickering barracuda.

"Mr. Fishpaw—"

"That would be 'Melvin,' okay by you?" The Chunky One set down his rum tankard and stuck out his right hand. It was roughly the size of a Baltimore Orioles catcher's mitt. Moon took the hand, which was still greasy from the shrimp. Fishpaw waggled it and Moon waggled back. "Nothing against you," the lawyer glared, "but *People* magazine broke every promise they ever made to me, and they humiliated my client. That's something a defense attorney doesn't forget." He was reaching for another boat-load of popcorn shrimp. "Anyway, that's the deal. So let's start over again, okay? What is it you want exactly, Mr. Moon?"

The stringer reflected for a moment. Blinked. "Well, as I mentioned on the phone, I'm trying to figure out what happened to Harry Zalenka. I assume you know who I mean?"

"Of course I do."

"Fine. In particular, I'd like to know why Harry washed ashore on Kent Island wearing all those diving weights."

Fishpaw stared at him for a while. Then he made a low, grunting sound somewhere on the back side of his tonsils. Was it laughter... or a subterranean digestive disorder? "So you want me to tell you about the tragedy of Harry the Z, do you? You're looking for the inside dope?"

"That's it," said Moon. "The dope. My editor wonders if there might have been foul play."

"Foul play?" The shrimp-eater squinted at him. "What a quaint expression. And why does this... this *editor* of yours suspect sinister doings?"

"Well, for one thing, Harry had a lot of lead tied to him when he drowned."

"Correct."

"Presumably, the lead made it harder for him to swim."

"That's an assumption—since scuba divers wear lead all the time—but go ahead."

"I've got a witness who says Harry was threatening to go public with some info about a huge Washington scandal, right before the end. Something involving espionage at the highest levels of the U.S Government. This same witness says you know about the scandal, too."

The big man guzzled his rum-Fresca, then emitted a leisurely burp. The stringer heard rivers at work in underground caverns, backed up and gurgling. "Tell me something, Moon."

"Sure."

"How much you know about quantum physics?"

Moon blinked. "Quantum physics? Not much. Nothing, in fact."

Fishpaw chuckled. "I thought so. Do you know enough to understand that the precise movement of atomic particles can never be determined with any certainty?"

"No, sir, I don't. I'm hazy as all get out on the atomic particles."

"Well, it's true. Your bosons, your muons, and your gluons—they're all whizzing through space night and day. But when you try to pin them down, it turns out they aren't actually *there*. Huh? Do I make sense? They don't really exist as particles; they're actually waves of energy. Or maybe they're both. They're particles *and* waves, at one and the same time. Huh? Can you dig it? What they are actually depends on how you choose to look at them.

"That's quantum physics, you see? That's your basic flying shitstorm, way down at the micro-level."

Moon showed no expression. "All right, fine," he said after a bit. "Quantum physics. Waves and particles, no prob. But where is this taking us, Melvin? How do the bosons and the muons relate to Harry Zalenka?"

The fat man grinned. He was obviously enjoying himself. "Think about it, Moon. According to the laws of quantum physics, the actual dynamics of ultimate reality are forever inaccessible to us. They're opaque, my man. They're unreadable. Just like poor Harry's death in the Chesapeake, they're a total enigma. How did that pathetic sad sack end up beneath the Fish O' the Day Pier? Better ask why the muon refuses to mate with the boson in the presence of the Strong Force.

"Can I buy you another Donald Duck?'

"Thank you, I'm fine." Moon was studying him carefully. "Is that all you can tell me about Zalenka? That the muons don't like the bosons?"

Fishpaw's double-wide face gaped open in what must have been intended as a smile. "Well, I do know that Harry wasn't a scuba diver. Never went scuba diving in his entire life."

Moon frowned. "Are you sure? Maybe he decided to give it a try, right before he vanished, and things didn't work out."

"Maybe. But it's one in a million. Is the boson contained in the electron-field, or has it escaped? Perhaps I could be more helpful if you told me what *you* already know."

The stringer meditated for a moment. "Okay. That won't be difficult, since I know so little. All I can tell you is, Harry washed ashore wearing the diving weights. And his sloop has vanished. He signed the boat out of a marina at Turkey Point, five days before he surfaced, and it hasn't been seen since. Oh… and his mother, Doris Zalenka—she lives in a Baltimore nursing home, but she's no help at all. She's senile."

He frowned for a moment. "That's it, Melvin. Beyond that, I don't know diddly, and that's the truth."

Fishpaw had begun to nod his craggy head. It was like watching one of the Adirondacks rise and fall. "Thank you for the eloquent summary, Moon. Terse and economical—I like that. But also woefully inadequate, I must say. As far as I can see, you haven't learned a fucking thing about Harry. I thought you were a *reporter*, pal."

"Well, not really," said Moon. "As I told you, I'm merely a news stringer. The magazine has its own internal reporters.

Real reporters. They work higher on the food chain. They take the info we stringers send them and they push it themselves. They're the actual reporters; we're nothing more than glorified clerks."

"I see. Still… your job is to stay at least a little bit ahead of the info-curve, am I right?"

"You are."

"And yet you've heard nothing about the bullet hole in Harry's head?"

Moon set his *Donald* down. "You're kidding."

"Not at all. Two different Coast Guard officers observed it, along with a sergeant from the Maryland State Police. It's fact, my friend. Check it out. Talk to the Coast Guard folks who answered the first call from the fishing pier. A small-caliber round is what I'm hearing: probably a thirty-eight."

"Holy shit," said Moon. "I just talked to that same state cop—Mazzoni—this morning, and he refused to comment. He gave me nothing. Are you saying Harry was shot in the head before he went in the water?"

"That does seem likely—given the fact that his skull had been ripped apart by a bullet."

"My God," said Moon. "This changes everything… Yang will shit a brick."

"Yang?"

"My editor."

"Oh. Well, you might also want to let him know –"

"Yang is a she."

"All right. Fine, then. I'm glad to hear that *People*'s an equal-opportunity shit-rag. Anyway, you might also want to let *her* know that the *Razzmatazz* has been found… and that the Coast Guard guys who boarded her discovered a half-eaten sandwich on a little table beside the wheel."

Moon was blinking faster now. "They found the boat?"

"This morning. It washed ashore just before noon, on the western side of Smith Island."

Moon peered at him. "Who found it?"

"A couple of bird hunters who were working the shoreline. They called the local fuzz, who quickly alerted the Coast Guard Station at Easton. The feds moved quickly, too; they were boarding the sloop within an hour. And what they saw was disconcerting, to say the least."

"I can't believe it," said Moon. "What did they find?"

"They found the wheel tied down carefully, and half a baloney sandwich sitting on a plate beside it. The mustard was still clinging to the knife. And there was a chart on the wheelhouse counter, as well. It was about half filled in, like somebody had been charting a course across the Bay." Fishpaw reached for another pile of shrimp. "If Harry Z killed himself, he must've done it halfway through his lunch—and right in the middle of writing in his daily sailing chart.

"And there's more," the fat man added after a bit. "The bottom line is, I knew Harry Zalenka very well, and suicide just wasn't his style. Harry was a bit of a paranoid, but he never would have done himself in—and you can quote me on that."

"Un-fucking-believable," said Moon. "How do you know all this stuff?"

Fishpaw smiled serenely. "I'm a criminal lawyer on the Eastern Shore of Maryland," he said after a bit. "Let's just say I have my sources."

Moon's teeth were hanging out. "But if he was eating a sandwich and working on a chart... wouldn't those facts shoot down the suicide theory? I mean, who jumps up from a baloney sandwich in order to blow his brains out?"

Fishpaw grinned. "You catch on fast, for a mere stringer. But you can't use the stuff about the boat yet—it won't be leaked to the media for another 24 hours."

Moon picked up his *Donald*. Drained it. "Again I ask: How the fuck do you happen to know all this good stuff?"

"No comment. But if you doubt me, watch CNN later tonight. The gunshot wound and the boat discovery are being leaked to Ted Turner & Co. as we speak."

Moon opened his mouth to say something, but then closed it. The Nokia had begun to burble. He reached into his jacket pocket. "Will you excuse me for a minute, Melvin? I have a teenaged daughter, and I don't like to miss her calls."

"I empathize. Take your time."

Walking away from the table, he punched *Calls*. But it wasn't Keera on the line.

"Moon, this is G. Gordon. Are you enjoying the *Rockfish Fra Diavolo*?"

Moon blinked slowly. His footsteps had led him into a deserted hallway full of bagged potatoes and onions. "Where are you, Gordon? How do you know we just ordered the rockfish? Actually, it hasn't arrived yet—we're still working on the popcorn shrimp. The main course will be along shortly."

"Oh, yes, the popcorn shrimp. Quite tasty, as I recall. Listen, you asked me to ring you if I turned up anything on Zalenka?"

"That's correct. And I'm amazed that you did."

"Well, I've got something."

"Really?"

"Truly. I do. And it isn't good. This is a live one, Moon. This one is *heavy*. There are some major players here, and you need to stay away."

"I hear you."

"Do you? I hope so. We're not talking Charlie the Tuna here, Moon. You need to understand: This is *Jaws*. Do you read me?"

"Loud and clear."

"Can I make a suggestion?"

"Go for it."

"You shouldn't be with the fat man. Not tonight and not ever. Do you catch my drift, Mr. Moon?"

"I do."

"If I were you, I'd finish my supper quickly, and then I'd depart. I'd also forget everything the fat man tells you, as quickly as possible. Take it from G. Gordon: That obese gentleman is not reliable—and he could get you hurt. As in, 'My spine doesn't work anymore.'"

"I understand."

"I also strongly recommend that you avoid his company in the future. There are forces at work here, Moon, major forces. Remember: *The winds are strongest near the eye of the storm.* Can you grasp that concept, witless one?"

"I can. I do"

"Fishpaw is the eye," said Liddy.

And the line went dead.

Moon stood motionless among the onions and potatoes for a few seconds. He was dazed, and his poor brain swirled with vertigo. Moving slowly, cautiously, he limped back to the restaurant table.

"Everything okay at home?" said Fishpaw.

"Yeah," lied Moon. "She's just fine. But oh, these teenagers! She wants $40 for a new sweater she spotted at The Gap. She'll worm it out of me eventually, but I'll stall her as long as I can."

Fishpaw nodded. "You parents," he said with a sigh. "You never cease to amaze me. I'm a lifelong bachelor myself. I don't know where people find the patience to raise kids, especially in these troubled times."

"It's a struggle, all right," sighed Moon. "All we can do is our best."

4. 'TWAS THOROUGHLY BRILLIG...

The rockfish was indeed superb, but Moon hardly noticed; his over-taxed brain seethed with a hundred questions for which he knew there would be no answers.

If the wheel had been locked on the *Razzmatazz* and a half-eaten lunch left sitting beside it...

If Zalenka had been working on a sailing chart shortly before he vanished...

And if he'd also been shot in the head...

Didn't that rule out suicide?

Or could the dead man have shot himself while leaping from the sloop's railing into the water? (*Scenario*: The gun sinks to the bottom, along with the weighted corpse; when the boat washes ashore without its owner, the insurance company is obligated to pay off for an "accidental" death.)

But what if Harry Z had been shot on the deck of the *Razzmatazz* by a visitor to the boat... then belted with diving weights and tossed overboard? Motive? It wouldn't have been robbery. And his killer (or killers) would've had to plan the whole thing carefully. Had they attacked Zalenka from a second boat? And *why*?

"Melvin, you were right. I must compliment the chef."

The gourmand nodded, but kept his gaze on the mammoth fish-platter before him. "I told you this guy was a genius."

"Can we talk about the gun?"

"We can. But it won't lead anywhere, because I've told you all I know."

Moon grimaced. "Your sources don't know if the bullet that killed Harry has been found?"

"They don't. Or if they do, they aren't sharing that info."

"No signs of a struggle aboard his sloop?"

Now the lawyer looked up from his meal. "Again, I have nothing for you."

Moon took a bite of tomato-laced rock. "I just don't get it. If we're talking suicide, Zalenka has to shoot himself while treading water. Or he has to jump from the deck, even as he pulls the trigger. It doesn't sound very likely. But if it was murder, what might the motive have been? Why would anybody want to kill a burned-out drunk living in a $40-a-week motel room?"

Fishpaw was digging a bone from an upper canine. "Maybe he knew something. Maybe there had been a terrible crime committed years before, and Harry knew about it. Maybe he was threatening to go public with his knowledge."

"That's a lot of maybes, Melvin." Moon put down his fork. "Are you suggesting that he'd learned something during his congressional term on the Hill? Look, I met this guy at the mo- tel... a guy named Spider? He knew Zalenka a little bit, and he said he'd been threatening to go public with some kind of huge spy scandal, just before he died."

Fishpaw produced a cheerful smile. "Who knows, Moon? Anything is possible, right? Just ask the physicists."

"George Yarnell—the guy at the motel. His nickname is Spider. He wears a Phillies baseball cap."

"Uh-huh. Sorry, but I never met him."

"He was nosy and he eavesdropped on you. He told me you visited Zalenka several times at the motel. Cabin Number Six. Spider said you sat on the porch and gabbed a lot."

Fishpaw didn't hesitate. "That's true," he nodded. "I did know Harry some, and I did visit him a few times at The Eve- ning Breeze. He'd done some investigative work for me over the years—nothing very involved and nothing terribly important."

Moon nodded. "Did he ever tell you anything about a project named Big Bird?"

The fat man gazed calmly at the scribe. "Big Bird? No. Wasn't he a character on Sesame Street?"

But Moon ignored that query. "Are you saying Harry never talked to you about how the engineering specs on Big Bird had been fed to the Russians by the mole inside the CIA?"

Fishpaw chuckled softly. "Good heavens," he said. "First Big Bird, and now a renegade mole? Sounds like poor Harry was spending too much time at the Children's Zoo. Did all of this come from that… that Spider guy of yours? What was his name again?"

"George Yarnell," said Moon. "A beat-up old redneck who lived next-door to Zalenka. Yarnell claims that you dropped by for a visit on the night before Harry disappeared."

The big man had stopped chewing. His face was a blank. "Well, part of that's true, anyway. There's no denying that Harry and I go way back. All the way back to the early eighties, in fact, when he was a brand-new congressman and I thought I was on my way to becoming Perry Mason. I always liked the guy, so I kept in touch after he lost his re-election bid. And when I heard he was down and out a few years ago, I sent him some minor-league investigative work from my law practice. A few small-time cases where he could earn a little spending cash, that's all.

"It was strictly routine stuff—cheating husbands, insurance fraud—and I threw it to him so he could pay the rent, that's all. And yes, it's also true that I dropped by The Evening Breeze a few times, but that was just to pick up some files and pay him for his work. Strictly routine. Maybe this guy Yarnell heard us talking about one of my cases."

Moon nodded. "I see. By the way, Spider also told me that Zalenka was a terminal alcoholic who'd begun to lose touch with reality."

"That sounds about right."

"He said Harry was a paranoid who thought Big Brother was always looking over his shoulder."

Fishpaw snorted. "The Z-Man had some outlandish notions, that's for sure. And yet he was also pretty goddam smart—a lot smarter than he looked, in fact. Until the drink caught up with him, Harry was one brilliant sonofabitch. He loved to read philosophy and poetry. Used to quote Lewis Carroll all the time."

"What, the *Alice in Wonderland* guy?"

"Yup. *Through the Looking-Glass*." The heavyset lawyer lifted his brass rum tankard on high and then recited:

" 'Twas brillig, and the slithy toves
Did gyre and gymble in the wabe.
All mimsy were the borogoves,
And the mome raths outgrabe."

"Nonsense rhymes," said the stringer. "Wasn't that the Cheshire Cat?"

"No, the Jabberwocky," said Fishpaw. He was studying the stringer carefully. "Moon, have you ever wondered what it's like to rub shoulders daily with the folks who work at the FBI and the NSA and the CIA?"

"I have, Melvin."

"Read Lewis Carroll. It's a helpful primer."

"How so?"

Fishpaw produced a guttural laugh. "One pill makes Alice large; another makes her small. Identities in flux. Everything up for grabs. Kind of like the gluon and the boson, huh? They're here, but they're *not* here, if you see what I mean? The quantum wave collapses, and all at once, there you are among the slithy toves."

"Uh-huh. Maybe I should slow down on the vodka," said Moon.

"Harry was a great fan of surreal literature," said Fishpaw. "Writers like Borges and Cortazar—he couldn't get enough of them. And he loved the Theater of the Absurd. Dramatists like Beckett and Ionesco… you know that play where the rhinoceros is loose in the house but nobody can see it?"

"I must have missed that one."

"And Kafka, of course. Harry really loved that story where the man turns into the cockroach and can't leave his bedroom."

"I imagine he would."

"He told me that story always reminded him of life in the House of Representatives." Fishpaw smiled. Then he dropped his napkin onto the table. "Mr. Moon, I think I've said quite enough for one night. What say we end our discussion—and begin the best part of our meal?" Now the fat man's smile was beatific.

"You gotta taste my guy's *maraschino* cheesecake—it's absolutely out of this world."

5. HELP FROM MR. KNIEVEL

Back on the road and headed for Baltimore, the stringer decided it was time to seek some professional advice. Having been spooked within an inch of his life by G. Gordon Liddy's terrifying phone call, he needed a realistic assessment of the dangers he faced on the Zalenka story... from a world-class expert on evaluating personal risk.

Approaching the Bay Bridge, he dialed the private number for a longtime pal.

"Knievel here. Talk to me."

"Evel! How you doing, my man?"

"Hey, Tommy! I'm *bueno, muy bueno.* Funny you should ask, because they just took the last metal pin out of my left leg yesterday morning. You know, I've broken 137 bones jumping all those Winnebagos over the years, and some of them had refused to heal. But they took hundreds of x-rays—and according to the docs, they're all healed up now, and I'm as good as new."

"That's terrific, Evel!"

All at once the world-famous stunt man was growling with laughter. "Shitfire, Moon, I'm feelin' so good these days... you won't believe this, but I been thinking about making a comeback! I mean it, too. I'm 57 years old, and that's no spring chicken... but hey, I dream about that San Francisco Cow Palace at least once a week. Were you there the night I jumped those 17 Greyhound buses and broke my spine in four places?"

"No... but I watched it on *Wide World of Sports*. As far as I'm concerned, that was the greatest single moment in the entire history of American dare-deviltry!"

"You *bet* it was, my man. They took me out of there in a full-length body-cast, but I got a 47-minute standing ovation. And so what if my backbone was completely shattered?"

Now it was Moon's turn to laugh. He'd never forgotten Knievel's explanation of why the big national promoters had been willing to hand him $1 million per leap: "Every time I took that motorcycle off the ramp, I had the wet diarrhea running down my leg. That's why they gave me the mill—because I was the only guy on earth who could stand the feeling of the wet diarrhea filling up his boot."

Moon understood that kind of terror—especially after hearing G. Gordon Liddy describe "death by No. 2 pencil." But this was no time for shared nostalgia. "Listen, Evel," he said hurriedly, "I need some advice. I've got a dead former congressman on my hands. They found this guy floating in the Chesapeake and shot in the head. G. Gordon's telling me to stay away from it—he says there are sharks in the water."

The stunt man gave a low whistle. "Liddy used that phrase?"

"Correct. Those were his exact words: 'Sharks in the water.'"

"Wow." There was a pause while Knievel meditated. Then: "Okay, I've got a couple of questions, if you don't mind. First, how long was the politico dead before they found the body?"

"Hard to say. Two, maybe three days. He washed up against a fishing pier."

"I see. And the weapon?"

"Small-caliber, probably a thirty-eight."

Another whistle. "Jeez, Tommy. That sounds like it might be a hit. Any of the major acronyms involved in the dead guy's past?"

"Yeah. I've got some scuttlebutt in which the dead congressman was claiming to have uncovered a mole, way up high in the CIA."

"*Jeez*, Tommy!"

"Right before he vanished, he'd been telling several of his colleagues that he had the goods on the mole—that he could prove the mole had given away the Pentagon's Big Bird spy satellite system. He was threatening to go public with his info—said it would blow the lid right off Washington."

There was a long pause as Knievel analyzed the risks. Then: "Tommy, I'm gonna tell you up front—I don't like it. Okay? It's toxic shit, for sure. Trust me: if there's a mole involved, the Company will stop at nothing to keep the story quiet. Can you still get out?"

"Probably not. Yang's pushing me hard on this one. The magazine's all over it. We're working it as hard as we can—and we're staring at a Friday afternoon deadline."

"I hear you. What's Yang's angle?"

"Oh, she wanted the usual horseshit at first. You know: The Sorrow and the Pity. The Heartbroken Women He Left Behind. But lately, she's also started pushing the investigative side—and she's got a real hard-on for *Murder, We Wrote*. She keeps asking why anybody would want to kill a guy who hadn't worked on Capitol Hill for more than a decade."

"He knew something," said Knievel.

"You mean Zalenka?"

"Right. He knew something important and he was about to go public—I can smell it."

"Fair enough. So what's my move?"

Knievel reflected briefly. Then: "Okay. If you can't ditch the story, you need to protect yourself while you work it. To do that, you need to create a phone conversation—on your *home* phone—where you point out that you're sending all your notes, every single thing you have, to several colleagues. They should all be editors at major U.S. newspapers, and they should be geographically scattered. Is that doable?"

"You bet. I've got five or six guys who'll hold the notes for me, no questions asked—journalists in K.C., Miami, Philadelphia... along with an editor at the New York *Times*... even though those self-important shits usually refuse to talk to other journalists. It's beneath their dignity, you know? But what's the strategy here, Evel?"

"It's simple, Moon: If you're working a story that might involve a Russian mole, you can be sure your land line is tapped. The spooks will be listening, you can be sure of that. By making it clear that you're sharing everything you've learned—every shred of information—with all these journalists scattered all around the country, you're telling the eavesdroppers that taking *you* out won't stop the story from breaking. What you're doing is buying yourself some protection—by spreading the wealth around."

Moon nodded. "Evel, I can't thank you enough. I owe you one, pal. How about another celebrity update on you in *People*? Maybe something like *Living Dangerously: Memoirs From the World's Greatest Stuntman?*"

"Now you're talking!" Knievel was growling happily again. "Hey, I've still got some gorgeous photos of that Snake River Canyon jump, never been released. Might make a nice cover, whaddya say?"

"Get 'em ready, Evel; I'll start priming the pump at the magazine."

"*Bueno*, Tommy, and *double-bueno*! And listen, before we hang up—I just thought of one more thing you might try. Why not call Henry the K and ask him if the Zalenka thing was a foreign hit? If you could eliminate the Russian mafia and the Sicilians as possible suspects, it would simplify matters enormously."

Moon sighed. "You're right. A great idea. But unfortunately, Henry has stopped taking my calls of late. Now that he's a network news commentator, he figures he doesn't need *People* anymore. Plus, his vanity was offended—the last time we wrote about him, we said that he'd been dying his hair—and that he talks through his adenoids."

"You're shitting me." Knievel sent up a loud guffaw. "Why, that egotistical little prick... and after everything you've done for him. How many times have you guys puffed up that war criminal during the past few years?"

"I stopped counting at six."

"That ungrateful little shitbox. But what else would you expect from The Trick's top-ranked ass-licker? Anyway, listen,

Tommy, I gotta run—the rehab therapists are here to work on my new platinum spinal disks. Cheers, bro!"

"Take care, Evel."

Heartened and encouraged now, the stringer produced a cheerful grin. With Evel Knievel behind him, how could he go wrong?

Feeling much better, he tossed the Nokia onto the dashboard and piloted the car into an open toll booth: *Chesapeake Bay Bridge, $5.50.*

6. THE MONSTER OF ENERGY

"How's it hanging, Ferg?"

The scowling Irish hulker looked up from his foaming tap. "Same as ever, Moon, same as ever. With heartbreaking regularity, one devastating tragedy succeeds the next. Will you be having your usual, then?"

"I will, Ferg. My usual vodka-*Donald*—and make it a double, *por favor*. And I'm sorry for your troubles. What's the matter, sidekick? Did another married woman turn you down?"

"Not a chance," groaned the mournful hooch-dispenser. "Who has time to chase the strange stuff these days? We've lost two bartenders this month, and I'm working 16-hour shifts." He slid the double-*Donald* toward the stringer. "I'm turning into a Japanese insect, like everybody else in this dogshit country."

"I hear you, Fenian warrior."

"Look at these hands, Moon-man." Ferguson raised them for display: two huge mitts, yellow-callused. "I haven't taken a blowtorch to metal in three weeks. And I call myself an *artist*?" His broad face radiated anguish.

Moon guzzled his *Donald* and groaned with empathy. When he wasn't running BAR, Ferguson was an iron-sculptor who tortured heavy metal into twisted, screaming faces. His jagged, eye-bulging heads were "emblems of the Monster of

Energy"—whatever the hell that meant. The grotesquely staring heads had deeply alarmed Baltimore's Art Establishment,
of course, and with good cause. Indeed, Ferguson himself was
afraid of them... yet he couldn't seem to put down his *artiste's*
blowtorch. During his off-hours from BAR, he labored inces-
santly in a cement-block garage he'd rented in Baltimore's
Lovegrove Alley.

"I'm totally disgusted with myself, Tommy," he wailed
now. "My iron heads are calling to me—calling day and night.
And where am I? What am I doing? I'm pouring cheap-ass
vodka—no offense—for a bunch of Crabtown lowlifes. Again,
no offense. Hey, you know and *I* know that I've got a gift for
sculpture—and that I'm gonna be called to account for that
gift, after the dust settles."

Moon shook his head. "Stop fretting, Ferg. Your time will
come. Perhaps an entity is gathering itself within you? For all
we know, a presence from the Beyond is striving to shape infi-
nite forms through your welder's torch. Perhaps Being Itself
will soon seek to manifest through the metal you bend and
scorch!"

Ferguson peered at him. "Jeez, you think so? Hey, I do like
what Henry Moore said: 'A sculpture is a wounded animal,
fighting to hold its space.' That guy was a real maniac, you
know? My iron heads... I want them naked and raving! I want
to feel the violence pouring out of them—the bitter acid of
their howling violence. Can you understand my passion,
Moon?"

"I can, Ferg. Better yet, I can *feel* it. But I'm struggling
with some difficulties of my own right now. My life hasn't
been easy of late. Yang handed me a journalistic time-bomb
the other day, and I'm just hoping it doesn't go off in my face."

Ferguson blinked slowly at him. "You mean that drowned
politician? Yeah, I've been watching that shit on CNN—looks
like a really weird story."

"It *is* weird. And it's dangerous. I'm afraid there are some
anomalies at work here, Ferg. Some perplexing discontinuities.
To speak frankly, I'm laboring beneath a cloud of cognitive
dissonance." He held up his tankard. "If it wasn't for my *Donald*, I don't know how I'd be able to endure."

The bartender was swabbing at a splotch of ruined Bud Light. Frowning. "You figure somebody whacked him, huh?"

"A distinct possibility. Apparently, the defrocked congressman believed himself to be in possession of some highly controversial info about an alleged mole in the CIA. That same mole, Zalenka believed, had been threatening to go public with his knowledge, right before he disappeared. And to make matters even more complicated, he turns out to have been a major-league fruitcake—one of those gibbering misfits who can find a conspiracy under every rock.

"According to a friend, Harry Z was convinced that a dark force had taken over the U.S. Government."

Ferg squinted. "Ronald Reagan, you mean?"

"No, even darker than Reagan, if that's possible. Harry had supposedly dug deeply into the assassinations of the 1960s. He claimed to have discovered patterns. He'd seen shadows on the Grassy Knoll. He insisted that Sirhan had never gotten within eight feet of RFK in the hotel kitchen... whereas the powder burns on RFK's skull showed that the gun had discharged at point-blank range."

"Weirdness," said Ferg. He was chewing on a toothpick, and glowering. "Spookiness in every direction."

"Something strange," said Moon, "in the neighborhood. Might I have a second *Donald*, do you think?"

Ferg went straight to work on it. Looked back over one shoulder. "Tommy, not to interfere, but I'm wondering if you might need a little bit of help in all of this—a little help with your personal security, I mean?"

Moon nodded. "An excellent idea, Ferg—but I don't have the funds that would be required to pay a bodyguard."

"Okay... but I was just thinking... we could always talk to my younger brother—remember Little Billy at the Bureau? Trust me, the G-Men understand these things. At the very least, maybe Special Agent Billy could advise you on how to stay safe... even while you go about reporting on the U.S. intelligence community?"

Moon thought about it. But then he shook his head. Lifted his tankard. Took a long, hard pull. "Not to worry, Ferg. I've been talking with G. Gordon and Evel about the security risks on the Zalenka caper… and they've both been very helpful. I don't need the FBI, at least not yet. But I've been keying into some spooky vibes, that's for sure—and they've got me a little bit rattled. Example: It seems that Zalenka didn't just 'accidentally drown' while wearing forty pounds of lead weights—he'd also been shot in the head. A provocative scenario, eh?"

"I'll say. Provocative in the extreme." Ferg glared some, and then brightened. For once, the mournful barkeep was actually sporting a grin. "You know, the more I hear about Harry Zalenka, the more I like the guy.

"I wish I could sculpt *his* head!"

WEDNESDAY

1. FANG'S FANCY FEAST

Two a.m.

A pair of eyes, electric-green, flared in the darkness of the stringer's empty apartment.

Then the front door swung open, the overhead lights flashed on—and the emerald-eyed creature emitted a snarl of primordial rage. He was crouching in front of the midget refrigerator, and he was truly pissed. All at once, Moon was staring into the greenish gaze of the world's angriest Maine Coon feline.

"Fang!" cried the mortified stringer. "Hey, I'm sorry, fella... I know you must be ravenous."

The chubby furball made a sneering sound somewhere deep in his throat.

"Honest, Fang... I got here as soon as I could." But the cat refused to meet his eye, and Moon could hear him thinking: *Yeah, sure you did. And I'm Arnold Schwarzenegger. Let's get moving with the can opener, shitass.*

Eager to feed his neglected roommate, the guilt-stricken Moon was already fumbling through the cabinet above the sink. "Let's see... I've got turkey-and-cheese chunks, steak tidbits... hey, how about a heaping bowl of Special Kitty Premium, Promotes Urinary Tract Health?

The cat snorted derisively. *Special Kitty? Brand X from the Happy Pet Center at Wal-Mart? Don't even think about it.*

"Wait a minute, Fang. We're in luck." He held up a royal-blue can marked with a glittering gold crest. "Fancy Feast Albacore—this stuff is top of the line!"

The Maine Coon grimaced once, and his whiskers quivered; it was as close as he ever came to a smile. While the cat wallowed in the high-end tuna, Moon went through the day's mail. Along with the usual overdue notices from Baltimore Gas & Electric and Chesapeake & Potomac Telephone, there was a pale gray envelope without a return address. Yawning with fatigue, he tore it open carelessly—then snapped to attention as the contents swam into focus.

Suddenly he was looking at a hand-lettered invitation written in jet-black ink:

Want to…
Know more…
About the Z?

Watch the O's…
Take on the Indians…
Camden Yards Stadium…
Wednesday, Aug. 16…
7:35 p.m.

(Ticket in your name at *Will-Call Window*)

Moon felt 14 hairs rise slowly from the back of his neck.

Fang felt it, too. Uncharacteristically, he'd stopped eating. Furry head poised above the bowl, the poker-faced feline was now staring directly at his owner, who could hear him thinking out loud: *What the fuck is this?*

Moon sat paralyzed for a few seconds. Then: "Can you believe it, Fang? I've been invited to Camden Yards to watch the O's tangle with the Tribe."

He turned the paper over… but found no writing on the other side. Blinking slowly, he'd begun to hold his breath without knowing it. Now he retrieved the pale gray envelope and studied it more closely. Except for his name and address, which had also been hand-lettered in black ink, there were no markings of any kind.

He stared at the front of the envelope for a few seconds and then sat upright in his chair... as he noticed that the letter-sized envelope bore no stamp. Indeed, there were no postage marks of any kind.

Which meant that this missive hadn't been delivered by the U.S. Post Office. Obviously, someone other than the mailman had slid this strange invitation through the crack beneath Moon's apartment door.

"Sonofabitch." Moon said the word out loud, and the cat's wet nose twitched in response. "Someone's been here, Fang. Earlier today. For all I know, that someone could be here still." Now he stood up. The cat's eyes followed him as he crossed to the door of the crapper and pulled it open. Toilet, sink, tin shower... and nothing moving. "There's nobody in the can, Fang; you can relax."

The cat peered at him with growing curiosity as he re-crossed the living room and yanked on the door of the single closet. He studied the ironing board. Then he studied the brown push-broom, along with the mop and bucket.

"Stay calm, Fang."

He went to the front door, opened it, and peered out. Nothing. He closed it and quickly attached the chain.

But these maneuvers failed to soothe. The hairs at the back of his neck had gone stiff with alarm by now, and his gut had begun to engage in some vertigo-laced acrobatics. *They're watching me*, he told himself. *They've been watching me ever since I visited Fishpaw. And now they want to watch a ballgame with me.*

"Someone has been here, Fang; someone has paid us a visit. Someone has offered to help me learn more about Z."

The cat lifted one eyelid slightly: *Your problem, pal, not mine.*

Moon resumed his perch on the chair. "I need some answers, Fang. Who sent me this invite, and why? How much does Fishpaw really know, and why isn't he telling? Why won't the muon mate with the boson in the presence of the Strong Force?"

But the Maine Coon didn't have any answers. Stuffed with prime filet of albacore, he was now stretched out full-length on his throw-rug. Apparently untroubled by the flickering spookiness that had arrived with the day's mail, the contented Fang was already snoring his head off.

Moon picked up the remote, flicked it over to 36: *CNN Headline News.*

For about ten seconds, he watched a man scrubbing himself in the shower while singing loudly: 'I smell clean! I smell clean!"

Then *Headline Update on the Quarter Hour* jumped into focus.

"There's been a shocking new development in the unfolding story about the former congressman whose body washed ashore in Maryland the other day.

"According to two different highly credible sources at the U.S. Department of Justice, the dead politician had been shot in the head at least once before his body floated to the surface of Chesapeake Bay on Sunday afternoon...."

Moon sat motionless in his chair while the CNN newscaster recited half a dozen other details, all of which demonstrated—with chilling clarity—that Melvin Fishpaw's inside information was for real.

Moon blinked slowly at the screen. What next? Apparently, Fishpaw's *bona fides* were 100 percent in order.

The fat man had gotten every detail right.

"Help me, Fang," said the stringer, after mulling his options for nearly an hour. "Help me understand what to put in my stringer file. What should I tell Madame Yang?"

But there was no reply. Oblivious, the obese feline snored on through the rainy night.

2. SECOND STRINGER FILE

***People* Stringer File #1512**
Date: *Wednesday, Aug. 16, 1995, Seven A.M.*
To: *YANG YANG, National Stringer Desk*
From: *T. MOON, Baltimore*
Subject: *Zalenkadrown, 2nd file*

POCOMOKE CITY, MD.—The tragic death of Harry Zalenka—a death that left his forlorn mother grieving help-lessly and broke the heart of his former wife, Meredith—took a shocking new twist on Tuesday evening, when investigators were quoted as saying the former congressman had been shot in the head before his body surfaced in the Chesapeake Bay on Sunday.

The 57-year-old politician had been hit once in the right temple with a round from a small-caliber pistol, probably a .38, according to information reportedly leaked by the U.S. Department of Justice to CNN late Tuesday. According to the news network, the one-term congressman from Maryland had been shot at close range—but investigators have not been able to determine whether or not the wound was self-inflicted.

This latest disclosure throws a pall of uncertainty over the cause of Zalenka's untimely death, according to investigators and friends of the onetime Maryland Democrat. The shooting occurred sometime after Zalenka's 27-foot sloop was checked out of a Chesapeake Bay marina—and before his body was discovered on Sunday afternoon. The sloop has not been seen since Zalenka signed it out of the Turkey Point marina last Wednesday.

"I knew Harry Zalenka very well, and suicide just wasn't his style," said a longtime friend in Pocomoke City, Maryland, last night. "Harry was a bit of a paranoid, but he never would have done himself in—and you can quote me on that."

The close friend, a veteran lawyer in this small town on Maryland's sparsely populated Eastern Shore, also noted that Zalenka's corpse had been belted with 40 pounds of scuba-diving weights when it washed ashore. "I want to know how a man wearing all those lead weights and swimming in the water could also shoot himself in the head," said the lawyer. "Are we to believe Harry jumped from the deck of his own boat—and then shot himself in mid-air?

"That's absurd. It's a preposterous scenario, as far as I'm concerned. If you look at the M.O. here, it's pretty obvious that somebody took Zalenka out. But why they might want to do that is beyond me."

The lawyer added that Zalenka had appeared "somewhat deranged" during the last few months of his life, as he sank into increasingly severe alcoholism. "The Z-Man had some outlandish notions, that's for sure," said the lawyer-friend. "The only word for them was 'bizarre.' And yet he was also pretty goddam smart—a lot smarter than he seemed. Until the drink caught up with him, Harry was one brilliant sonofabitch. He loved philosophy and literature... used to quote Lewis Carroll all the time."

The Maryland attorney went on to suggest that Zalenka had become "totally paranoid" in the months before his body was discovered at the Catch O' The Day Fishing Pier on Kent Island, located about 30 miles east of Baltimore. According to the friend, Zalenka believed the federal government had been taken over by a vast conspiracy—by a criminal cabal which had actually launched an invisible *coup d'etat* with the assassination of JFK, way back in 1963.

"Harry was a major-league fruitcake, especially toward the end," said the grieving Melvin Fishpaw, "but I'll never believe he was suicidal.

"Something here just doesn't add up."

END MOON STRINGER FILE #1512
8/15/95

3. EYEBALL TO EYEBALL
WITH THE DONALD

Having shipped his stringer file off to Gotham City—and while waiting for the inevitable explosion from Yang Yang—the deeply troubled stringer was determined to take Evel Knievel's advice and consult with one of the world's savviest political analysts.

But no sooner had Moon walked into the lobby of the super-exclusive Café Bonaparte—located on Wisconsin Avenue in the heart of Washington's upscale Old Georgetown neighborhood—than he found himself confronting a very angry man.

"You're late, Mr. Moon!"

No, that wasn't Donald Trump talking—it was actually the *maitre d'*, the legendary Jean-Paul Lafitte, clad as usual in a full tuxedo that included a freshly picked blue orchid peeking from the top buttonhole in his perfectly fitted jacket.

"I'm sorry, sir," said Moon, who as always was struggling to overcome his neurotic fear of restaurant waiters, whether French or not. "The traffic was brutal all along M Street."

"*C'est vrai,*" said Monsieur Lafitte, "but that does sound a bit like an excuse—and I think we know how Mr. Trump feels about *those*?" He sent the stringer an Arctic smile, then reached for a menu that was larger than the Washington Post. "If you will kindly follow *moi*?"

Moon trailed along meekly, while Monsieur Lafitte led the way past a tinkling piano bar where a Chopin *etude* was being tinkled by an elderly woman with fiercely dilated nostrils. A moment later, The Donald was looking up from the *Cote d'Agneu* Roasted Duck Leg *Confit* he'd already ordered and been served.

"You've kept me waiting more than 19 minutes," snapped the real estate mogul, whose straw-yellow hair was stiff with his legendary impatience. "Make no mistake, second-rater: If you worked for me, you'd already be *fired.*"

"I understand that," said Moon. "I'm very sorry."

"Sorry's just another word for loser," said The Donald. "By now you'd have been shit-canned, dispatched, thrown out on the street, dumped, deep-sixed and doomed to spend the rest of your life in a shelter for the unemployable, you totally pathetic nobody, you."

"Traffic on M Street," said Moon.

"Traffic, my ass," said The Donald. "Sit down, you despicable zero."

"Is *Monsieur* drinking anything?" sniffed the *maitre d'.*

"Yes, thank you," said Moon. "*Monsieur* will have a punchbowl-sized vodka on the rocks. Hah-hah!"

The *maitre* stared at him, poker-faced.

"Just joking," said Moon. "A double Stoli on the rocks with a twist of six-month-old lime from the southwest coast of Antigua, *por favor.*"

Lafitte stared. "What? *Qu'est-que c'est? Por favor?* The *maitre's* eyebrows were soaring. Do you mean *s'il vous plait?*"

"Speaking Spanish to a French *maitre d'?*" snapped Trump. "How fucking vulgar can you get? This is the Café Bonaparte, you dickhead. I'm telling you now: You wouldn't last thirty seconds, if you were working for me."

Moon sat down. He meditated for a moment. I'll have the *Moules Frites*," he said to the Maitre, "with an order of fries on the side."

The Maitre gaped at him. "Fries?"

"*French* fries," said Moon. "This is a French restaurant, isn't it?"

"My God," said Trump. "You're ordering French fries in a French restaurant? I'll tell you one thing right now: If I were publishing *People* magazine, you'd be fired in a New York City heartbeat, you lackluster toad. You'd be out the door so goddam fast –"

But Moon cut him off.

"Donald, I have some good news for you."

"You do?" Trump ran one hand through his huge straw-yellow hair. As usual, he looked like a super-sleek possum in the middle of being electrocuted. "What's up, Tommy, my man?" And he cut loose with his toothiest smile. Suddenly, his world-famous rage had been replaced by cheerful bonhomie. But why was he suddenly so happy? Did he sense what was coming next?

"Remember that *Up Front* celebrity kiss-ass puff-piece you wanted us to write about you at *People*?"

"Of course I remember it," snapped Trump. "I've been waiting months for that celebrity kiss-ass puff-piece to be published, you know that."

"Well, it's about to hit the newsstands. *Trump: A Day in the Life of an American Genius.* I've already finished most of the reporting on it—and you're going to love the results. This puff-piece will completely neutralize all those recent stories in the liberal press about your vicious gouging of your tenants and your vampire-like destruction of thousands of desperate human beings at your various far-flung casinos where people are fired every minute on the minute, 24/7."

Trump nodded. "Good, good. Glad to hear it. It's high time those baseless fictions were put to rest!"

"Trust me," said Moon. "Once this blockbuster runs, your PR problems will be over forever. The *People* extravaganza we have in mind could even set the stage for a Trump run at the White House—and I'm not just blowing smoke."

Once again, Trump produced his hideous, just-out-from-under-a-rock smile. "That's very encouraging," he purred. "But I have a question."

"Ask it."

"Why are you such a lying, utterly treacherous piece of human offal?"

Moon gazed calmly at the mega-tycoon. "Well, I'm *not*," he said.

"You've been promising me that story would run for the past six months, you disingenuous sneak-face. But every week when I pick up the Time Warner rag, *nothing*."

"Calm down, Donald. It took us a few weeks to pull all the art together."

"Bull hockey. Stop pulling my chain, liar."

"Ten days," said Moon. "If that six-page sweet-old-butt-kisser isn't out in ten days, you can feed my liver to one of the sharks in your penthouse aquarium. How's *that* for a guarantee?"

The Donald took a bite of his *Cote d'Agneu*, then settled back. "All right, the clock is running. Now what can I do for *you*? I'm a very busy man here."

Moon looked at him. "Donald, I need your guidance. Everybody knows you're the smartest ruthless business tycoon in America –"

"Make that in the *world*."

"Okay, the smartest ruthless tycoon in the world. And that's exactly why I need you, Don. I need your guidance, your wisdom regarding a reporting issue that's come up at *People*. I'll give it to you in a couple of sentences."

"Shoot."

"I've got some reliable information that a mole at the CIA stole the engineering specs for our largest spy-satellite system and fed them to the Russians. That's one sentence."

"I'm listening," said Trump. "Give me the second sentence."

"My sources also tell me that former Maryland congressman Harry Zalenka, who drowned in the Chesapeake Bay a few days ago, knew about the mole and was threatening to expose him, less than a week before Zalenka vanished from his sailboat and was then found dead wearing 40 pounds of diving weights and shot in the head."

"Goddam, that was a long fucking sentence, Moon. What's your question?"

Moon blinked slowly at the real estate czar. "What's really going on here and what should I do about it? As a reporter, I mean?"

Trump pursed his huge lips, then frowned. "No problem," he said. "Here's the deal: the mole is trying to cover his tracks. He's hoping Zalenka was the only guy on Capitol Hill who knew about his treachery. If you can convince him that *People* is on his trail, he'll crack—and he'll probably confess. After that, you'll be a national hero, and you'll probably win a Pulitzer."

"All right," said Moon. "I like all of that... but what do I *do*?"

"It's simple," said Trump. "Here's my advice, in exactly 20 words: March into the CIA headquarters and announce loudly that they're harboring a mole and that you intend to sniff him out."

"That's 21 words," said Moon. He thought for a moment. Then: "Okay, I like your plan, Donald, but I'm concerned about one particular aspect."

"Name it."

"What if the mole doesn't crack, but instead issues orders to have me erased?"

Trump snorted impatiently. "Jeez, Moon, are you a *reporter*, or what? If the mole sends in an assassin, simply outwit him. Become proactive... you kill *him*. Cripes, do I have to lay it all out for you? If I didn't know better, I'd be tempted to believe you're chicken-shit!"

The stringer nodded. "Okay, got it. Outwit the assassin, and instead of being killed, I kill him. That's brilliant, really. I can't thank you enough, Donald. That's terrific advice, and I'm glad to have it."

"Anytime."

"*Monsieur*?" Now the two diners looked up; Moon's *Moules Frites* had just arrived, along with a side order of fries. Glaring, the outraged *Maitre* slapped them onto the table. "*Pommes frites*, just as *Monsieur* ordered."

Moon nodded and then put his hand on the platter of fries. He gave them a good feel. "Not hot enough," he told the *Mai-*

tre. "Please take these suckers back to the kitchen and micro-wave them another minute or so, will ya, Frenchie?"

Thoroughly impressed by the stringer's sheer brass balls, The Donald cut loose with his enormous trademark grin.

4. ONLY 48 HOURS TO DEADLINE!

"Moon, have you lost all touch with reality?"

The stringer closed his eyes. *Goddam that chink slut to the depths of fiery, shrieking hell.*

"Hi, Yang!"

"Don't 'hi' me," snapped the stringer chief. "I just read your latest file, and by the middle of the second paragraph, I was holding my nose. Why are you reporting shit from CNN as if it were *your* shit?"

Moon gripped the Nokia harder. His tortured knuckles were bone-white. "Wait a minute," he wailed at the Asian sadist on the other side of the microwave towers. "I gave you plenty of new shit, Yang! What about all those quotes from Fishpaw? CNN didn't have *any* of that stuff! And so what if I made half of 'em up?"

Now Yang barked with ugly laughter. "How many times have I told you to never bullshit a bullshitter, Moon? Those were blind quotes—you didn't even *name* the guy, you spineless dweeb. No wonder you made them up!"

Moon closed his eyes. "You know I can't out Fishpaw," he shouted at the microwaves. "I can't talk about what he knows, either—trust me. But he's got the inside skinny, for real. How am I sure that's true? Well, for starters, he told me about Zalenka's gunshot wound *before* it ran on CNN!

"He also let me know—strictly off the record—that the missing sailboat has already been found... although the news hasn't been leaked to the media yet. And here's some more inside dope for you: he says the Coast Guard guys who boarded the abandoned sloop found the wheel locked, with a half-eaten sandwich on a plate and a sailing chart that had been partially completed."

Yang was silent for a few moments, and Moon pictured her sitting in her black-painted cubicle on the 37th floor, snickering sarcastically. "That sounds pretty dramatic, the way you tell it," she sniffed. "So tell me: why the fuck isn't that good stuff in your stringer file, Brainless One?"

Moon groaned. "Geez... will you please think it *through*, Yang? If Zalenka really *had* sniffed out a mole, and if Fishpaw really *was* his only friend and confidante—then it's only reasonable to assume that the fat man's being watched. Think about it. The mole knows that somebody *else* knows he gave away Big Bird... and that the 'somebody else' may very well have told his best buddy about the theft. No wonder Fishpaw insisted that our interview had to be off the record! Am I making any sense?"

"You're making non-sense, you moron. Look, I want you to put all that good shit from Fishpaw back *on* the record. Call him and tell him that, do you hear me?"

"Yang... I'm sorry, but I can't do that."

"Why not, you uncooperative sonofabitch?"

"I gave him a promise, Yang. I gave him my word."

She snorted. "Word, *schmerd*! This is the real world, you raging a-hole. This is the world of *journalism*—fuck him!"

"Yang, I'm very sorry –"

"Sorry, *schmorry*! Call that grotesquely obese shyster and tell him we're quoting every word he uttered to our 30 million readers—and if he complains, tell him he's goddam lucky to be appearing in *People*, period. Do you know what most lawyers would give to be featured in the world's most popular magazine?

"After you straighten Fishpaw out, get busy following up every lead he gave you. Talk to the Medical Examiner about the body... and talk to a few of the congressmen who knew

Zalenka on Capitol Hill. Interview the Coast Guard guys who
boarded the abandoned sloop and tell me what they found.
Then start working the CIA. Find the mole and get him to confess—and I might be able to keep Tolliver One-Two-Three
from cutting your throat on Monday.

"Get it done, and do it now—we're less than 48 hours from
deadline, you fumble-witted cretin, you!"

Moon's mouth fell open, and he began to beg: "Please,
Yang, be reasonable. Don't you see –"

But the line had gone silent. The microwaves had all evapo-
rated—and Moon was talking to no one but himself.

Again.

5. HOW 'BOUT THEM O'S?

He arrived at the stadium—Oriole Park at Camden Yards—at 7:14 p.m. It was a balmy evening in mid-August… with a fat gold moon hanging over the right-field bleachers. Hurrying across the vast, concrete expanse of the South Parking Complex, he watched a yellow hot dog wrapper bouncing along the pavement. The late-summer breeze felt damp, greasy against his face. What was that odor of decay, that faint hint of sulfur in the air? Ah, yes: he was sniffing the toxic pollution drifting in from the Eastside Trash Incinerator, located only two miles to the east....

Tonight's starting pitcher for the Indians… Number 55, the American League all-star, Orel Hershiser!

Gut clenched with anxiety, the stringer listened to the booming echo of the loudspeakers as he joined the milling throng outside the stadium's main gates. Once again, his over-taxed brain was seething with a hundred questions, each more troubling than the last. Who had sent him the anonymous invite to this evening's contest with the Cleveland Indians? Would there really be a ticket waiting for him at the Will Call Window? And how would the dark-side operatives who were obviously watching him choose to make contact?

There was only one way to find out.

Gritting his teeth with determination, he turned his steps toward the neon-lit window at the giant playground's Camden Street Entrance.

Amazed, a moment later, he watched the attendant pull a monogrammed envelope from the stack before him. "Oh boy, lucky you!" sang the ticketmeister in the orange O's jacket. "You're gonna be sittin' in Terrace Box 54, right behind third base.

"You're so close to the field that if Cal Ripken's playing third tonight, you'll be able to chat with him between pitches!"

After thanking his benefactor, Moon stole a quick look at the brightly colored pasteboard in his hand:

TERRACE BOX 54, SEAT 12. $44.

As always, he was amazed by the high cost of the ticket. With more than 100,000 Baltimoreans living beneath the federal poverty line, it was hard to believe the local ball club could charge more than $40 to watch 18 grown men stand around scratching their balls and periodically spitting on the vivid green turf of the playing field.

But that was the reality. Go... O's!

Here are tonight's starting lineups... brought to you by Mercantile Bank and Trust of Baltimore!

Moon eased into his deeply cushioned chair and then took a look around. The first pitch was still ten minutes away... but the nearby seats in his Terrace Box were filling up fast. Pulse racing, he watched two CEO-types stride toward their perches in an adjoining row. They were lean, strong-jawed figures in nearly identical pinstripe suits; one even carried a gleaming leather valise. Corporate guys, he decided, and obviously harmless. Directly behind them sat a middle-aged man and a little boy. Father and son? There would be no harm from that quarter, either. As the minutes ticked past, Moon was frantically studying the fast-growing crowd of baseball fans in search of the government spook who might be hiding among them....

No luck. Nothing out of the ordinary. He twisted uneasily on his seat. Perhaps the secret agent would wait until the game had gotten well underway… in order to draw as little attention as possible?

O's fans, please rise now for the singing of our National Anthem!

They were in the middle of "gave proof through the night"—when Moon felt a light tap on his left shoulder. Startled, he flinched away badly… and then felt thoroughly foolish.

The tapper was an elderly woman, a grandmotherly figure with soft blue eyes and snow-white hair.

The Anthem ended.

"Mr. Moon?"

He stared woodenly at her for a good ten seconds. "Correct," he finally said.

"I'm Mrs. Feeley," said the newcomer. Somehow, she'd managed to creep into the nearly full Terrace Box without his noticing her. Now she sank onto the empty chair beside him. She was smiling happily… a tiny, gentle-eyed old lady in a royal- blue pillbox hat

Batting leadoff for the Indians tonight… Number 7, Centerfielder Kenny Lofton!

"Mr. Moon," said Mrs. Feeley in a low voice that didn't carry more than six feet. "I see you have no program. But that's okay, because I've brought you one."

He looked over, saw her smiling cheerfully at him. The hat was tilted at a jaunty angle; it featured a rakish yellow feather and a row of gleaming pearl buttons.

"Here," said Mrs. Feeley. "I suspect you'll find this helpful." Now she was holding out what looked like an ordinary, orange-hued game program: *Oriole Magic '95!*

He took it. "Thank you," said Moon. But his voice broke on "you," as he gulped in a huge mouthful of air.

"You might want to look at page 25," said Mrs. Feeley. "It will help you figure the game out!"

He nodded and then sat motionless in his chair for a few seconds. The world was truly a strange place, was it not? It was. He turned the pages slowly.

The program fell open at page 25—BOXSCORE—a page ordinarily left blank, so that those fans who wanted to could chart every play during the contest.

But this BOXSCORE form wasn't blank. Instead, a few words had been printed in dark blue at the exact center of the page.

Z
MADE
VIDEO

TIME
TO
PICK
UP
THE
LAUNDRY

His mouth fell open. Z had made a video? A video of what? And why were they providing this remarkable fact to a journalistic pipsqueak like Moon? And where was that video? Was it still on the scene, or had it gone into the drink with Harry? And if it was still around, who was going to retrieve it? Questions, questions...

He ruminated. Then he flinched again... as Mrs. Feeley leaned toward him. Now she spoke from one corner of a frozen smile, her lips not moving. "The video will tell you everything," she said. "But you have to find it first."

Moon swiveled his head to gape at her. "*I* have to find it? Why me? I'm just a *People* stringer!"

"Don't look at me," said Mrs. Feeley. "Look straight ahead."

He did his best.

"We think he completed that project fifteen years ago," she said without moving her lips. "Then he tried to blackmail somebody with it. But the blackmail attempt blew up in his face. The bad guys called his bluff and decided to take him out. Harry knew they were coming for him, and he hid the blackmail evidence right before they got there."

Moon pondered. "Who are *they*, Mrs. Feeley?"

A buzz went through the crowd—Kenny Lofton had just lined a frozen-rope single into straightaway center.

"Who was he hiding the evidence from?" said Moon.

"We don't know," said Mrs. Feeley.

Moon deliberated. "All right then," he said. "I'm pretty sure you can't tell me, but I'll give it a try. Who is 'we'?"

"I can't tell you."

Batting second for Cleveland... Number 11, Shortstop Omar Vizquel!

"And what *laundry* is this?" Moon groaned. "What laundry are we talking about?"

She didn't hesitate. "Whiz Cleaners," she murmured. "It's on Harford Road at Cold Spring Lane. Northeast Baltimore."

"What time?"

"Doesn't matter. Anytime tomorrow."

"What will I find there?"

"An explanation."

"Why can't *you* explain?"

"I don't have all the parts. They'll give you the rest at Whiz Cleaners."

He shook his head. Moaned with a mixture of animal fear and maddening frustration. "Have you ever heard –"

"Look straight ahead."

"Do you know a guy named Fishpaw? A lawyer in Poco-moke City?"

"Never heard of him. Sorry."

Now she was on her feet.

"Tomorrow," she said. "Whiz Cleaners. Good luck, Mr. Moon."

The crowd groaned as Omar Vizquel pulled a three-and-one pitch down the left-field line and into the 14th row of the bleachers.

And she was gone. Somehow, she'd simply vanished from the scene.

Indians 2, Orioles 0.

But Moon wasn't keeping score. *Holy shit,* he told himself, *Harry must have made a videotape of the mole. Somehow, I'm going to have to find it.*

6. SAMSA DECODED?

Driving back toward the Dump, with his poor brain reeling, Moon clung to the Nokia for dear life.

"This is Melvin. How you been?"

"Thank God you're there!" the stringer shrieked into his cell phone. "Melvin, I need your help. I need your advice. There have been… developments."

A brief silence on the other end. Then: "Developments, you say? What kind of developments?"

"I went to an Orioles game."

"Good for you," said Fishpaw. "How'd they do?"

"Hey, I didn't go for *fun*. I was *told* to go. I received this anonymous letter last night at my apartment. Somebody bought me a ticket."

"Glad to hear it. The prices they're charging to watch a big-league ballgame these days—absolutely outrageous!"

"Goddammit, Melvin, you're missing the point. Somebody shoved a letter under my door. Told me to drop by the Will Call Window at Camden Yards. I wound up in Terrace Box 54—and then this little old lady showed up. Mrs. Feeley. She wound up in the next seat. Wore a funny-looking hat with a yellow feather—and she gave me a program. When I opened it, there was a message in there saying Zalenka had made a videotape."

"Really? How interesting. What kind of videotape?"

"How should I know? The kind of tape you play on a VCR—I assume that's what it was. Did you ever hear anything about a tape that Harry might have made?"

"Nothing." There was another pause; Moon could hear the wheels grinding inside the fat man's head. "Did this... Mrs. Feeley person say what was on the tape?"

"Nope. Not a peep. She suggested I drop by this laundry in Baltimore tomorrow. Whiz Cleaners."

This time Fishpaw was silent for a full half-minute. When he finally spoke, Moon heard a new note of fear in his voice. "Did you say Whiz Cleaners?"

"I did."

"You're sure?"

"I am."

"Moon... I'm not going to tell you your business. You're an experienced journalist, and I'm sure you know what you're doing. But you might want to think it through, before you visit Whiz."

"Really? Why so?"

"Whiz Cleaners is a certain kind of domicile. I'm not going to tell you what kind, out of respect for the computers that might be listening to our conversation. I don't want *you* to name that type of domicile, either. Do you understand?"

"I... I think so."

"I'm going to ask you a question. Do not answer it aloud."

"Okay."

"You just went to an Orioles game. Okay... if a baseball umpire calls a runner 'out,' he makes a particular call. What's the *opposite* of that call—do not answer aloud!"

Moon clamped his mouth shut. *Safe.*

"So that's the kind of place we're talking about," said Fishpaw.

Moon had begun chewing his lower lip. *Safe house.*

"Moon, I want to congratulate you," said Fishpaw. "It seems that you've now graduated to the major leagues of espionage."

The stringer shook his head. "Goddamit... all I wanted were some sound bites, Melvin! Somehow, I've been dragged into a whole lot of crazy government shit I can't even understand. At this point, the only thing I can figure is that Zalenka must have been blackmailing somebody high in the government. Maybe there's something incriminating on the videotape he made. Mrs. Feeley seemed to be suggesting as much. She told me that Harry probably tried to hide the tape, right before he disappeared.

"What should I do, Melvin? What's going on here, really?"

The fat man emitted a deep, avuncular chuckle. "Twas brillig, Moon, and the slithy toves did gymble and gyre in the wabe."

"That's not funny. I'm in deep shit here."

"Wish I could help—but I doubt that I know any more about all of this than you do." He chuckled again. "I did come up with one helpful clue, however. Remember at dinner the other night, you asked me about that government acronym you found scribbled on the counter at the motel?"

"Sure. SAMSA."

"Right. Well, I don't think it *is* an acronym. I've computer-searched the records of every federal agency during the past fifty years, and no sign of any SAMSA. But the name got stuck in my head—and this morning in the shower, I suddenly *got* it.

"It's the last name of a character in a famous story by Franz Kafka. Gregor Samsa—he's the guy who turns into a roach in *The Metamorphosis*."

"Oh, really?" Moon's heart was rapidly sinking. "Thanks, Melvin... but I've never read the story."

"Better head for the library. Think about it: Maybe Zalenka was trying to leave a clue behind. Maybe he was trying to point us toward something in the story, as a way of telling us where the videotape might be hidden. It's a thought, anyway."

Moon sighed and shook his head. Suddenly, he felt so exhausted that he could barely keep his eyes open. But at least he was finally home; with a bleary yawn, he pulled the Sprint into its parking space outside the Dump.

"Thanks, Melvin. Gregor Samsa. I'll keep it in mind."

7. A MIDNIGHT VISITOR

He hit the living room light switch and got a surprise.

No sign of his surly feline. He looked around anxiously. Why wasn't the X-large Maine Coon lunging at Moon's shins, while fiercely demanding his long-overdue dinner?

"Fang? Hello? Where are you, wild thing?"

With the key still in his hand, the stringer stepped deeper into the Dump. Then, as his eyes slowly adjusted to the glare from the naked overhead light bulb, he received a vicious shock.

An intruder sat in the NaugaLeather easy chair!

Home invasion!

The housebreaker was a smirking man in a slanted Fedora... a sneering man who wore a jet-black, carpet-sweeper mustache.

Moon's eyes went to the burglar's hands. Fascinated, nearly hypnotized, he watched those hands at work. *No. It can't be.*

But it was. The hands of the invader were slowly, relentlessly sharpening a No. 2 pencil. Moon watched in horror while the man in the imitation-leather chair held the yellow scribbler up to the light—so that Moon could eyeball its stiletto-sharp point.

"Hello, Moon."

"Hello, G. Gordon."

"It's been far too long," said the renowned cat burglar, "since you and I sat down and had a really good talk."

"You're right."

"I understand you watched the Orioles blow another ball game tonight," said G. Gordon. "A real bummer, huh? What's wrong with those guys, anyway?"

"They've got no left-handed relief pitching," said Moon. "That's the word on ESPN, anyway."

Liddy sighed. "My, my, my, what a shame. Well, that's baseball, isn't it?" He shook his head sadly. "Pitching is everything, they say." With the index finger of his right hand, he gently smoothed the carpet-sweeper. "Moon, do you know what I could really use about now?"

"What's that?"

"A cup of fresh-brewed tea. Got any Earl Grey?"

"I do," said Moon. "Actually, I wouldn't mind a cup myself."

"Excellent," said Liddy. He set the No. 2 pencil down on the coffee table beside him. "And while you're preparing that beverage, I'd like to explain a few things, if that's okay by you? I'd like to lay out our basic ontological situation, you and me, what say ye?"

"Fair enough," said the stringer. "Cream and sugar?"

"Just a teaspoon of sugar, please."

"No problem. By the way, where is Fang?"

"Oh, is that what you call him? Your cat friend is locked in the crapper. He's fine. I just wanted to keep him out of harm's way."

"Thank you," said Moon. "But I'll have to let him out—he hasn't eaten since early this morning."

Liddy nodded. Moon crossed the tiny apartment and pulled open the crapper door. The big cat waddled through the doorway and confronted his roommate. His green eyes were pools of glittering rage. Those eyes vibrated with a message in italics, a message for Moon's eyes only: *You are a blight on my entire life.*

"I'm sorry," said Moon.

"Nothing to be sorry about," said Liddy.

"Actually, I was apologizing to Fang."

"I see. Go ahead and feed him then, no problem."

"All right, thank you," said Moon. He stepped toward the counter, toward the waiting jumbo can of Bumblebee. Fang's green eyes began to fill up with the usual greedy lust for fish flesh.

"Let's get a few things out of the way," said Liddy. "First of all, we don't have to pretend about Zalenka and the videotape, do we? I think we both know that Harry Zalenka made a tape back around 1980, and the tape had something to do with a mole working high up in the U.S. Government. Are we agreed on that much?"

"Agreed," said Moon. He was spooning tuna into Fang's plastic bowl.

"I think we also understand—both of us—that Harry Z was threatening to go public with what he knew about the mole and about Big Bird. It seems likely that the stuff on the videotape was the proof he needed to make his charges stick. He was hoping to collect a very large bundle of greenbacks, either from the Russians or from the mole himself. But instead of scoring a big payday, poor Harry got whacked."

"Sounds on target to me," said Moon. He'd put the kettle on and sparked the flame; now he was lowering an Earl Grey tea bag into a chinaware mug.

"I don't know how much of that you got from Fishpaw," said Liddy, "but I'm very sorry you chose to listen to him. I warned you to stay away from the fat man, and you chose to ignore my warning. You're either foolhardy or crazy—or maybe both.

"But none of that matters now. What *does* matter, from my point of view, is making sure the video doesn't end up in the wrong hands."

Moon looked calmly at the celebrity Watergate bungler. "Gordon, have you been involved in all of this from the very beginning?"

Liddy thought for a moment. Then he smoothed the carpetbagger with his index finger. "Moon, I'm surprised you don't know by now: I'm involved in *everything* that happens within our federal government. Can you grasp that simple fact, benighted magazine stringer? Really. If it's occurring in Washington and it involves skullduggery, you'll find me there. Can we just settle on that fact and move on?"

"So noted, counselor."

"Okay then, here goes. Let me start by providing you with a very quick backgrounder. First of all, I'm sure you must know—as a veteran journalist, I mean—that the average American bear, here in the Year of Our Lord 1995, doesn't have the faintest clue about what really goes on in Washington. True?"

"Absolutely," said Moon. "No question."

"The average bear in Minneapolis or Atlanta—he comes home from work, pops the top on a Bud, flops down on the sofa, watches Dan Rather... and comes away with three or four clichés about the so-called 'workings of democracy'. And those frayed, shopworn clichés are all light-years removed from the reality."

Liddy reached over and picked up the pencil. Smiling benignly, he studied its razor-sharp point. "Your average bear never dreams, for example, that the world of inside-the-Beltway Washington D.C. is actually engaged in permanent warfare."

The kettle had begun to bubble merrily on the rusted stove.

"Your typical bear has no way of knowing that the internecine rivalry between the FBI and the CIA, let's say, is actually much more intense—and much more lethal—than, say, the rivalry between the USA and the newly enfranchised Republic of Russia." He sighed again, sighed and frowned. "Let's face it: all of the federal acronyms are fighting around the clock for bigger budgets, bigger influence at the White House, and a bigger footprint in the sad little world of the bought-and-paid-for national news media.

"Still with me?"

"I'm hanging on every word," said Moon.

"Good. So let's move now to the present tense. Let's say, purely hypothetically, of course... let's say that there has, indeed, been a mole burrowing his way happily through the highest layers of our most vaunted spy agency in recent years.

"And let's further say that the biggest enemy of that vaunted agency—J. Edgar's internationally renowned Bureau,

I mean—somehow happened to get wind of that mole's trai-
torous deportment some time back. What then, Mr. Moon?
What then?"

The stringer set the steaming mug of *Earl Grey* down in
front of the former Langley operative.

"Well," he said. "I imagine there would be a struggle of
some sort."

"Very good," said Liddy. "You're right on it. You're perspi-
cacious in the extreme, Mr. M." He lifted the mug and took a
tiny sip. "Now… what *kind* of struggle do you think that might
be?"

"Well, I imagine it would be a struggle to find and publish
the videotape. The Bureau would be struggling to expose it,
and thus to expose the mole… while the Company would be
doing its best to keep the damning evidence hidden—in order
to protect its gigantic, taxpayer-funded yearly budget."

"Brilliant," said Liddy. "Isn't this fun? I salute you for that
diamond-sharp analysis." He watched the stringer settle warily
onto the edge of the apartment's only other chair. "So where
are we? Ah yes, we're in the midst of a ferocious struggle between two government agencies. The public thinks they're
both engaged 24/7 in fighting off the Russkies and the Chinks,
but we know better. We know that their greatest struggle is
against each other—always and forever, world without end."

"Amen," said Moon.

Liddy sipped. "All right, then. So far, so good. Let's move
on to our next topic. Let's talk about a major chapter in that
struggle—the struggle over the bona fides of one Gregor
Yevchenko. Tell me, Mr. Moon: do you know who that gentleman was?"

"I think I do."

"Enlighten me."

"He was a KGB colonel who defected to the U.S. from the
Soviet Union back in the 1960s."

"Excellent. Do you know about the battle over his bona
fides?"

"Only what I read in the newspapers."

"Which was?"

"I read that there was disagreement inside the CIA about whether Yevchenko had really defected... or whether he had come to the West in order to spread disinformation, as a triple spy."

"Outstanding, Dr. Moon! Do you recall reading that the effort to verify the Yevchenko bona fides had served as the major battleground between two factions in the Company—the Richard Helms faction and the James Jesus Angleton faction?"

"I recall that, but only vaguely."

"Understandable. Just one more question, please: Do you remember what Yevchenko's major message was—the key message he brought to the West?"

"No."

"Let me help you. He came bearing one critically important piece of information: the assertion that the Russians had not been involved in the JFK assassination in 1963. Helms believed him. But not James Jesus. For more than a decade, those two fought to prove that their opposed versions of the Yevchenko story were the correct versions. And it was around that struggle that the modern identity—the essential *Weltanschauung*, if you don't mind a bit of German—of the modern CIA eventually took its shape."

Now Liddy lifted his cup. He sniffed and savored. "This is excellent *Earl Grey*, Moon."

"Thank you."

"I know you've been caught up in all this silly crap about Big Bird," said the disgraced spook. "But what if I told you that Big Bird was merely a *legend*—merely a convenient cover story designed to hide the real activities of the mole?"

"That would be pretty dramatic, all right."

"Well, my friend... that's precisely what I *am* going to tell you. In point of fact, the theft of Big Bird by the mole and its subsequent leakage to our Russian friends is simply a legend. It was designed to hide the real activities of the mole."

Moon nodded. "Which were?"

Liddy set the cup down again. "Ah, how much I wish I could give you a simple answer to *that* query, scribe! But once we move toward the region of Yevchenko's bona fides—and the KGB's alleged non-culpability in the JFK horror—the atmosphere grows increasingly murky. The landscape becomes positively... *metaphysical*—no other word will do. Of course, Angleton admitted as much himself. You know that he studied literature and wrote poetry at Yale?"

"I do."

"Angleton was the smartest person in the world, Moon."

"So I've heard."

"No one on this planet has ever been smarter."

"I'm sure you're right."

"*I'm* pretty goddam smart," said Liddy, "but even I could not hope to keep up with Angleton."

"I don't doubt you in the least," said Moon. "You are certainly one smart White House cat burglar. But Gordon... can you help me to understand where all of this is *taking* us?"

"Absolutely," said Liddy. He picked up his tea again. "Let me summarize our basic situation for you, okay? First, we know there's a tape, and that Harry Z hid it somewhere before he went for his deep-dive in the Chesapeake. Next, we can be fairly certain that the tape contains something—some record of a meeting or an exchange of some kind—that sheds major light on the identity of the mole and on how the mole fits into the struggle over Yevchenko's bona fides.

"In this swarming welter of possibilities, what can we be sure of? For me, the answer to that question is a simple one— given my own position on the federal food chain. Above all, it seems to me, one principle reigns supreme: *That videotape must never see the light of day!*"

The profound silence that followed went on for at least 20 seconds.

Then Fang sent up a leisurely burp. His supper ended, he had stretched out on his throw rug and put his furry feet into the air. Soon he slumbered.

Liddy, meanwhile, was holding up the super-sharp No. 2 pencil.

"Mr. Moon," he said quietly, "I hope you understand how serious I am in saying that the tape must remain out of sight."

"I think I *do* understand," said the stringer.

"I hope you're giving thought to the possible consequences that could follow"—and he gave the No. 2 a good waggle—"if you were to locate the tape and disseminate in publicly."

Moon nodded. "Don't worry," he told the mustachioed breaker-and-enterer. "I'm scared shitless."

"Good," said Liddy. He was on his feet now, and striding toward the door. But then he turned back. "Before I leave, I think I should give you one last piece of information. I'm sure it will surprise you."

Moon stared. "What?"

"You remember the autopsy Dr. Pangborn was supposed to do on the body?"

"You mean… the autopsy by the Maryland medical examiner?"

"The same," said Liddy. "Well, you might be interested to know that the autopsy never took place."

Moon frowned. "It never happened? Why not, Gordon?"

Liddy sent the stringer an icy smile. "Because the body never reached his office, that's why. It was intercepted en route– by armed agents from Langley—and then transported to the offices of the Company."

"You're kidding."

"I'm not. Within an hour of its arrival at CIA HQ, poor Harry's corpus was cremated in the CIA's own onsite crematorium."

Moon was blinking furiously. "I'm stunned, G. I'm amazed. And I'm unbelievably frightened!"

"You should be," said Liddy. "Do you finally understand what you're playing around with, you imbecile? Do you finally see how fucking *dangerous* it is?"

"I do. I do!" Moon's face was a mask of raw terror. "Look, I'll tell Yang that I simply refuse to cover the CIA side of the story," he barked at the departing dark-sider. "As a stringer, my most important function has always been gathering weepy sound-bites from women whose hearts have been broken—and from this moment forward, I'm going to *restrict* myself to that function."

Liddy turned at the door. Smiled once. Smoothed the carpet-bagger with one index finger. "For your sake, Tommy Moon—I hope that's true!"

And then he was gone.

THURSDAY

1. "YOU'VE GOT
THE WRONG GUY, PAL"

By 8:30 the next morning, Moon had already arrived on Capitol Hill. It was time—finally—to meet one of Yang's most insistent demands... that he interview a few more of the longtime politicos Harry Zalenka had worked with during his single term in the U.S. Congress. Today's mission would be a simple one, uncomplicated by cloak-and-dagger complexities. As always, Yang had described the task with naked bluntness: "Get a few color quotes about dear old Harry from some of those assholes on the Hill."

The first of the assholes would be one Nolan Fitch Montgomery—the esteemed Senior Democratic Senator from Virginia. Already a veteran four-term congressman when Zalenka was elected in 1980, the drawling, silver-haired show-boater from Norfolk had reportedly become a close pal of the Maryland freshman. Unlike Zalenka, however, Montgomery had managed to hang onto his electoral perch throughout a brilliant career. A gifted speaker, he'd used his down-home eloquence and his leonine good looks to win several House terms... and had then mounted a successful statewide bid for the U.S. Senate in 1982. By 1995, he was a fixture on the Hill—a veteran, third-term senator who'd recently nailed down the coveted post of Chairman of the Senate Intelligence Committee.

Nolan Montgomery would be the most important target on Moon's interview list today. But the *People* fact-chaser knew he had little hope of actually speaking to the Democratic bigwig, who was far too busy to waste precious minutes on a mere magazine stringer. But so what? All Moon needed, really, was a sentence or two from the senator's press aide, Abe Bechtel. Actually, he didn't even need *that...* but merely Bechtel's permission to run a totally predictable color quote that would mean nothing, anyway. The meaningless quote would read something like this:

"I knew Harry Zalenka well," said Democratic Senator Nolan Montgomery, while remembering the dead congressman's two years in the House back in 1980. "Harry was a dedicated lawmaker with a knack for working with colleagues on both sides of the aisle, in order to craft legislation aimed at making life better for everyone in America. He will be greatly missed."

The passage was total horseshit, of course, but it was *required* horseshit. Quite frequently, in this kind of scenario, the reporter would simply make up the quote in advance... then submit it to the press aide for approval. This procedure saved time for everyone involved—but in order to get it done, you had to nail down a signoff from the aide. And to accomplish *that*, you usually had to "drop by" the aide's office in person—since the busy PR functionary would never return a phone call from a mere reporter who merely wanted a meaningless color quote. From the point of view of the press aide, there was nothing to gain from making the call, so why bother?

That was the basic drill on color quotes: to get the two meaningless sentences, you had to show up in the politico's office and then French-kiss the PR chief's butt.

And he would. Moon's description of the process, which he frequently expanded on at BAR, was simple and direct: "If you're covering the Hill, you gotta eat at least one frozen turkey turd per day. It's unavoidable—no way around it."

And today would be no different. After fighting the usual 25-minute battle for a parking space on North Capitol Street, the stringer finally managed to dump the Sprint and then loped toward the congressional office buildings that loomed like a squadron of stone monoliths on the rainy horizon. By eight-thirty, he was hustling along Constitution Avenue toward the main entrance of the graceful old Richard Russell Senate Office Building and the fifth-floor offices of Senator Nolan Fitch Montgomery.

As he strode past the gleaming Doric colonnade and the giant arched windows that formed the architectural signature of the hundred-year-old landmark, Moon was asking himself a fretful question: *What if I choke on the turkey turd and don't get the signoff for my made-up quote?*

Stepping aboard the mahogany-paneled elevator for the ride up to the fifth floor, the stringer was also grilling himself for at least the tenth time about the wisdom of his visit to the Hill. Was he taking a risk by showing up unannounced like this? The senator was a specialist in intelligence with a Top Secret Clearance, after all—and the sudden disappearance and death of his former congressional pal must have set off more than a few alarm bells in the Washington spy network. Better watch your step, Moon warned himself, *because you never know who might be watching*. Groaning inwardly, he watched the gold-plated elevator door rumble open and then began shuffling down a long, marble-lined hallway toward Number 522.

Approaching the door—and the frozen turkey turd—he took a deeply frightened breath. But before he could put his hand on the brass knob, he got a major shock... when the massive oaken door suddenly swung open on its own.

A sixty-something gentleman was at that moment exiting the senator's office. He carried a pebble-leather valise and he wore an expensively tailored, pinstriped suit. Was he one of the senator's senior aides? Or maybe one of his high-powered and well-connected constituents?

"Good morning," said Moon, just as the elegantly clad older man looked him full in the face.

Moon froze. *Holy shit.*

It couldn't be... but it was.

All at once, the stringer was staring into a pair of very familiar blue eyes. He was staring, in fact, at the same craggy forehead… at the same scarred nose… at the same prominent lip-mole he'd seen on the old man at *The Evening Breeze Motel*!

Moon stopped dead in his tracks. "Excuse me," he said.

But the staffer had already passed him by now.

Moon turned. Blurted: "Mr. Yarnell!"

Now the elder statesman in the elegant suit was looking back over one shoulder. He was frowning. Glaring. "I beg your pardon?"

"Aren't you George Yarnell? I'm a journalist… a stringer for *People*… and I'm sure I interviewed you a few days ago in Trappe, Maryland!"

The staffer man glared again. His hostile gaze radiated scorn and anger, in equal amounts. "Yarnell?" he said. "Sorry, I've never heard of him. You've got the wrong guy, pal."

And he turned toward the elevator.

Moon stood flatfooted, watching the brass doors clatter open. A moment later, the man with the briefcase was stepping inside.

Bullshit, Moon told himself. *Bullshit! That's George Yarnell, no question about it. I'd remember that scar—and that mole—anywhere. That's the Spider, man!*

He turned. He ran for the stairs. He nearly fell twice, plummeting toward the street. But when he finally reached the lobby… desperate for a second look at the man in the elegant pinstripes, he was too late.

He whirled to confront the blue-uniformed security guard at the electronic scanners. "Excuse me… did a man in gray pinstripes… a man with a black briefcase just come through here?"

The security guard stared back at him, expressionless.

"Mister, do you know how many people come through that door every hour?"

2. A PANICKED CALL TO FISHPAW

"Melvin, it's me. There's weirdness loose, barrister. There's major weirdness running wild on Capitol Hill!"

"Tell me something I don't know," said Fishpaw. "You sound like you're starved for oxygen, Mr. Moon. Calm down. What happened—did you wander into a Republican congressional caucus, or what?"

"Something far worse—I ran into the Spider. I can't believe it. I was on my way to Senator Montgomery's office—chasing a signoff on a horseshit quote, nothing very important—and there he *was*. He had on a really expensive suit… looked like a thieving tax lawyer… so at first I assumed he was an oil industry lobbyist, you know? But this was no lobbyist; that was the *Spider*. George Yarnell, remember? The guy at the motel? The old hillbilly who told me to call *you*?"

There was a pause on the other end, while Fishpaw digested the weirdness. Then: "Are you sure? Spider on the Hill? It sounds a tad improbable… but in a world where the gluons come in and out of existence at the bidding of the Weak Force and the Top Quarks, why not?"

Moon took a gulp of air. Multiplying frantically in his overheated mind, the questions were stacking up like jets at O'Hare. "Melvin, do you realize… Montgomery was a close pal of Zalenka's back in the day?"

"I do realize that," said Fishpaw.

"And now, Senator Montgomery is... what?"

"A shit-brained Democrat from the Old Dominion State?"

"Yes, he's that, of course," barked Moon. "But more importantly, he's the goddam chairman of the goddam Senate Intelligence Committee! Which means he spends his days eyeballing all kinds of dark-side shit from the Valley of the Spooks. He's got a Top Secret Clearance and friends scattered throughout the world of Washington intelligence. CIA, DIA, NSA, NIS, FBI, MIC, MCIA, ONA, ACIC, AFOSI—Montgomery is wired to every one of those secret agencies, along with the intelligence services run by all of our major allies worldwide.

"Now ask yourself: If George Yarnell is working for Montgomery—and I'm absolutely positive I saw him in the Russell Building just now—then the senator must have dispatched him to The Evening Breeze Motel in order to –"

But Fishpaw cut him off. "Easy, Moon. You're speculating wildly, and you know it. We aren't sure the guy you saw was Spider, for one thing. Maybe it was his identical twin, and the twin went into politics? And even if it *was* Yarnell, that doesn't prove anything. Maybe he was just doing some reconnoitering on his own, just checking out the traffic at the motel that day."

"Get real, Melvin! Ask yourself: If Spider was sent there by Montgomery... and if he was pretending to be a mere harmless yokel... what was he *after*? Remember: *he's* the one who planted the story about the mole that Zalenka had supposedly uncovered. For that matter, he's the guy who sent me to *you*.

"So here's the sixty-four-million-dollar question: Why did Montgomery want *People* magazine to start digging into the story of the mole?"

Moon waited, but his heavyset friend had once again fallen silent. And then, out of the utter blue, it hit him.

"My God, Melvin—they're watching *both* of us. They steered me to you... so they must think you know where Zalenka hid the tape."

More silence from the seedy lawyer on the other end of the line.

"Melvin... no hard feelings... but I gotta ask: *Do* you know where Zalenka hid that tape?"

"No!" wailed Fishpaw. "Listen, Moon, I swear to you on my mother's eyes—he never told me. Okay, okay, I don't deny that I held back a few things during our rockfish dinner the other night. I did talk with Zalenka about the mole... and also about the video he made of Montgomery. I've never actually seen that tape—but I know for a fact that it shows the senator meeting with one of those famous KGB guys who defected to our side. I also know the meeting took place in 1980... and that whatever's on there will prove two things: first, Montgomery's playing for another team; and second, that turncoat shitster is the one who gave the Soviets Big Bird!"

Now it was Moon who fell silent, while his feverish brain raced through the questions and answers.

Q. If the Montgomery-led spooks really believe that Fishpaw knows the whereabouts of the tape, why don't they just kidnap him and sweat him until he talks?

A. They can't do that—because they know he's being protected by somebody very powerful.

Q. Who has enough muscle to stop one of the major federal acronyms from torturing an ordinary citizen, if they need to do it to obtain info?

A. The only outfit with that kind of power has to be... *another acronym!*

Stunned, Moon had nearly dropped his cell phone. Suddenly, everything was becoming crystal-clear.

"Melvin," he said with a grunt of pure amazement, "I think I'm starting to figure some of this out. The mole can't grab you because he can't be certain you won't tip off one of the *other* intelligence agencies in Washington, which might then produce the tape and go public with it. At the same time, he isn't positive you even know where the tape *is.* Which means that he and his people can't touch you—all they can do is *spy* on you!"

Silence for a moment. Then a low whistle of admiration from the Large Man. "Moon, I think you're actually starting to get it—and I'm thoroughly impressed. Are you sure you're only a lowly *stringer?*"

"I am, Melvin, but thank you. And here's one more fascinating conundrum for you: How does SAMSA fit into all of this? As you kindly pointed out, we now know that SAMSA is the name of the main character in the Kafka short story. But how does that matter? Why would Mr. Z scribble the name of a man who becomes a roach on his motel countertop? Do you think Zalenka might have been using the story as some sort of *code*? Was he hoping he could lead somebody to the location of the tape by getting them to analyze the story and *break* that code?

"Melvin, I'm asking you flat out: Is the key to the puzzle somehow contained in the language of *The Metamorphosis*?"

There was a long pause... and then Fishpaw sent up another deep, avuncular chuckle. "Moon, have you ever heard that famous saying: 'A fool can ask more questions than a wise man can answer?' How the fuck would *I* know if there's a secret code hidden in that famous short story? Hey... I'm just a shyster-lawyer living in small-town Maryland!

"As far as I know, there's only one man on this planet smart enough to figure all this shit out—and that man is Henry the K."

Moon's eyes widened with hope for a second... but then he groaned out loud. "Yeah, well, thanks for the suggestion, Melvin... but I'm sorry to report that Henry the K hasn't been answering my phone calls of late."

"Really? Why not?"

"He's pissed off at me. You see, we've been promising to run a flattering profile of him in *People* so he can jack up his fees as a global consultant who teaches financiers how to avoid paying their fair share of taxes... but the damn thing hasn't hit the stands yet, and he's really gotten impatient."

"Oh, too bad," said Fishpaw, sounding mournful for a moment. But then he brightened: "Look. Why don't you drop by and pay him a visit in person, Moon?"

"In person? Get real, Melvin. Nobody on earth can visit Henry the K in person. He's completely invisible. No fixed address, no phone number, nothing. He just *is*."

"I can put you there."

"You're kidding."

"Nope. It's my only claim to fame. As a shyster lawyer with Washington connections, I'm privileged. I don't know why exactly. I guess I'm just the kind of guy that an international master-criminal like Henry the K would want to keep in touch with. Anyway, I've got his current address right here in my Rolodex. You ready?"

"Unbelievable," breathed Moon. "Fire away."

"You'll find Henry the K at the Whiz Cleaners laundry on Harford Road and Cold Spring Avenue in Baltimore."

Moon opened his mouth to reply, but nothing came out.

Whiz Cleaners? It was the safe house!

3. ONLY 32 HOURS TO DEADLINE!

"Moon, I've read through your latest file."

"And?"

"I see evidence here of mental instability."

"You do?"

"I do. *Lots* of evidence. Do you mind telling me what's going on? If you're actually able to do that, I mean?"

Moon took a breath. "Ahhh... explaining it all would be difficult, Yang. Things have become, shall we say, a bit *complicated*?"

"Try."

"Okay. Now, just for starters... it seems that George Yarnell—remember that old guy I interviewed at the motel?"

"How could I forget that yokel?"

"Well, it seems he's actually working for the chairman of the U.S. Senate Intelligence Committee."

"You're shitting me."

"I wish I was. Make that *were*—the subjunctive, right?"

"Moon, would you please explain to me what the fuck our story is about?"

"I'll try. Apparently, Zalenka had made some sort of videotape back around 1980, and the tape showed a mole at work in the U.S. intelligence establishment."

"Apparently, you say?"

"Best I can do right now, Yang. Apparently, Zalenka was down on his luck, drinking heavily, and in his desperation he tried to blackmail the mole—who promptly took him out. They popped him on board the *Razzmatazz* apparently, then weighted him down with the diving weights. But the body apparently inflated with decomposition gases and he bobbed back up."

"That's three 'apparentlys' in one paragraph, you asshole. Did the Maryland Medical Examiner confirm that scenario or not?"

"The Medical Examiner never even looked at the body, Yang. As it turns out, Zalenka's body was intercepted en route to Dr. Pangborn's office—by armed emissaries from Langley. He's already been cremated in the CIA's own on-site crematorium, according to my sources."

Yang snorted so loudly that it hurt Moon's ear. "Your *sources*? Don't make me laugh. Who *are* these sources, you basket case?"

"You know who, Yang. Liddy. Fishpaw. Oh, there's also a Mrs. Feeley involved. I have no idea who she represents. Or is it 'whom'?"

Yang was silent for a moment. Then: "Listen to me, you quintessential moron. Today is Thursday, ten a.m. Our deadline on *Zalenkadrown* is 5 pm tomorrow. That's 31 hours, nitwit. Stop pulling your pudder and start putting together a story outline—or I'll let Tolliver One-Two-Three take away your livelihood. Do you hear me?"

"I do, Yang. And I'm hoping you won't give up on me. Because I think I'm close to a breakthrough. I really do."

"How so?"

"I'm closing in on the tape. All I have to do is figure out the secret code that's hidden in Franz Kafka's story, *The Metamorphosis*. Do you know that one? It's about a salesman in Prague... he turns into a roach. Or is it a beetle? I can never tell those two apart. Actually, I think a lot of people who aren't entomologists frequently confuse –"

"Shut up, dickweed, and get to the point: How is the Kafka story going to help you find the tape?"

"Harry left a word scrawled on a counter at the motel: SAMSA. Fishpaw thinks that word is the key to the entire puzzle."

"He does?"

"Correct. Figure out the code in the story, and you'll know the location of the videotape that exposes the mole who gave away Big Bird. You'll also know who killed JFK and the other guys who were killed in the sixties—King, RFK, Malcolm X, you name it. This thing is big, Yang—it's going to blow the lid off Washington!"

"Really? That would be nice for the magazine. Maybe we could even continue to pay you. But if all of this stuff is so hot, why haven't you figured the code out yet?"

Moon sighed and shook his head. "I *can't* figure it out, Yang—I'm not smart enough. Liddy and Fishpaw... they're way smarter than I am, and they can't figure it out either. There's only one man who can do that: Henry the K—and I'm headed there now. I've found an address for him—a working address!—and I'm en route there as we speak. He's in Baltimore. He's in a safe house—Whiz Cleaners—in the northeast section of the city. I've been promised an interview."

"By whom?"

"Mrs. Feeley."

"Oh, yes. Mrs. Feeley."

Frowning, Moon swung into the passing lane, then zipped past a blue-painted truck: *Muhly's Bakery*. The Sprint's puny engine whined in protest. "Yang, I'll phone you right after I meet with Henry. If he's as smart as everyone says he is, I'll walk out there with the exact location of the video, and we'll be on our way to a Pulitzer."

Yang chuckled deep in her throat. "For your sake, Moon, I hope that's true."

4. AT WHIZ CLEANERS

At first glance, Whiz Cleaners appeared to be nothing more than an ordinary neighborhood dry cleaning establishment in northeast Baltimore.

But first glances often deceive.

For at least five minutes, Moon walked back and forth along the Harford Road sidewalk, eyeballing the layout. The laundry was contained inside a flimsy-looking, stucco-fronted row-house. Above the paint-peeling façade, a wooden sign had been painted in now-faded lettering:

WHIZ CLEANERS.

From his vantage point on the sidewalk, the stringer could observe the dim figure of an elderly woman who was bending over an ironing board. Each time she moved her hot iron, a tiny cloud of steam jetted forth: *Pssshhhh!*

It had begun to rain a little… a thin, yellowish rain (full of sulfur from the nearby Eastside Trash Incinerator) that trickled along the gutters, en route to its final and poisonous destination at the bottom of the Chesapeake Bay.

Moon knew he couldn't postpone the showdown any longer.

It was now or never.

With halting, tremulous steps, he limped along the wet sidewalk, then mounted the four steps that led up to the doorway of the cleaning establishment.

He pushed the door open, and a little bell went: *Ding.*

The woman at the ironing board looked up from her work. Moon stared at her, and then he caught his breath.

"Hello, Mrs. Feeley."

She smiled. Her mild blues eyes were soft and friendly. She looked like the world's kindest grandma. "Hello, Mr. Moon. I hope you've been having a pleasant day."

"Oh, yes," said Moon. "Very pleasant. Thank you for helping me last night at Camden Yards."

"Oh," she said. "That was nothing, Mr. Moon. I was happy to be of assistance."

"And thank you for asking me to stop by."

She smiled. "You're always welcome here, Mr. Moon."

"One of my sources tells me that this is the headquarters for Henry the K."

"Roger that, Mr. Moon."

"Is he the reason you asked me to stop by?"

"Of course he is."

"Amazing. It seems that while I was looking for him, he was looking for *me.*"

"Reality can be very strange at times," said Mrs. Feeley. "Why do you want to see Henry, Mr. Moon?"

"Henry is the smartest man on the planet," said Moon. "He's the only man who can help me now."

"Really? Why so?"

Moon looked calmly at her. "I'm trying to solve an extremely challenging puzzle."

"I see. Well, Henry's certainly good at that. But before I take you to him, may I ask a couple of questions?"

"Of course."

She was still ironing the shirt she'd been working on when he entered the room. The iron slid back and forth, jetting a bit of steam on each pass: *Pssshhhh!*

"First of all, we wanted to know how you happened to send Yang an email that included the word 'SAMSA'."

Moon stared at her. "You know Yang?"

"We do."

"But she's... she's a magazine editor."

"Is she? Actually, Yang wears several hats. She's a very complex figure, and also very patriotic, I might add. But let's get back to SAMSA, may we? I believe you sent that word to Yang as part of a memo?"

Moon thought for a moment. "I did. It was part of what we call a 'Stringer File'. Nothing very complicated, Mrs. Feeley. I simply reported that I'd found the word scribbled on a counter-top at the Maryland motel where Zalenka had lived, right before he disappeared."

Mrs. Feeley smiled. Moon liked her smile—the red in it glowed softly, comfortingly. "Mr. Moon," she said after a bit, "this next question might strike you as odd, but I'm wondering if you have an opinion on the assassination of John F. Kennedy?"

Moon blinked slowly. Stupidly. "The president?"

"That would be him, yes. What do you think happened in Dallas that day?"

Moon deliberated. He could hear a jackhammer pounding away, somewhere in the distance. There was always something going on in the city. He felt a trickle of fear. Like a trickle of dry sand at the back of his throat. "Well, I don't know much about that event, not really. I mean... based on what I've read, it seems likely that Oswald acted alone. A nut case. You know? A little guy with a box of carry-out fried chicken in one hand and a mail-order rifle in the other.

"But I don't have any inside information, if that's what you're asking."

She smiled warmly again. "Inside information?" she said. "That's very quaint. Now... we were also wondering if, in your various travels, you'd ever heard of a Russian gentleman named Yevchenko?"

Moon swallowed back some more of the sand-trickle. "Only what I read in the House Assassinations Committee report," he said. "Gregor Yevchenko defected from the KGB in 1964, and he claimed to be bringing proof positive to the West that Oswald had not been one of theirs. Am I remembering the sequence correctly?"

Mrs. Feeley reflected for a minute. "You're fine," she said. "Very good, Mr. Moon. You do have a good memory. Now… just one more thing. That word, SAMSA?"

"All right," said Moon. "I'm not sure where this is going, Mrs. Feeley. Actually, I came here today in order to ask Henry the K that same question!"

She smiled. "All right, fine. And I'm sure he'll help you answer it. But for right now, we'd just like to get *your* take on that puzzle."

"My take?"

"Correct." Pssshhhh!

Moon watched her iron slide back and forth over the garment. Could things get any stranger? He was talking in Baltimore with a woman named Mrs. Feeley, talking about five letters he'd read on a motel countertop. "Well," he said after a bit, "I'm sure you remember that SAMSA is the name of the alienated guy in Franz Kafka's story, *The Metamorphosis*."

"Oh, yes," said Mrs. Feeley. "Gregor Samsa."

"Uh-huh," said Moon. "Well, he wakes up one morning, and he's a cockroach."

"Roger that," said Mrs. Feeley. "And?"

Moon peered at her. "And… what?"

"What do you make of that fact?"

"Well," said Moon. He was frowning now, and trying hard to put some words together. "I think the story might be about… you know, the modern world?"

"Uh-huh."

"You know, this Samsa guy, he's a salesman, out on the road all day, and he's doing his best, but he can't help noticing how strange everything is."

Mrs. Feeley was gazing intently at him. "That's a very thoughtful assessment, Mr. Moon. Does Yang share your interpretation of the story?"

Moon's mouth hung open. "Yang? I don't… we don't really work at that level, Mrs. Feeley. Really, we're just trying to get the magazine out. It's a weekly, you know—we face some killer deadlines."

She had cocked her head to one side now, and one eyebrow had flared. She looked like an extremely intelligent tropical bird who'd been stumped, at least for the moment.

Pssshhhh!

"But surely, Mr. Moon... surely the fact that Zalenka had written that word down on the countertop—I mean, that was a key element in your Stringer File, was it not?" *Pssshhhh!*

Moon saw that his left shoelace had come undone and bent to tie it. "Not really," he said. "For us, that name was just a detail, at least at first." He looked at her. "I think it might help, if I try to explain how we actually work, at *People*.

"You see, we're not actually trying to understand reality at the magazine. We're far too busy for that. That would be way too ambitious for us. Actually, we're just trying to pull together all these... you might think of them as prose cartoons. Okay? I know I do. Harmless little cartoons... quick little fact-bites, we call them. But the hard part is that our lawyers have to be able to defend those cartoons, in case we ever get a libel suit.

"So the key thing is... you have to gather the facts for the cartoons, and you have to make sure they're accurate, at least on the surface, so that your lawyer-guy can protect Time Warner in a lawsuit. Time Warner, you know who they are?"

"I do."

"Really, the whole process has very little to do with reality, Mrs. Feeley. It's all about building a legal case around the little fact-bites."

Mrs. Feeley was watching him carefully.

"So... if you were thinking, like"—he was doing his best to get to the bottom line—'Okay, these *People* reporters are out there trying to capture reality,' well, that wouldn't be very accurate. Okay? So Yang wouldn't really be asking me, like, 'What is the meaning of SAMSA?' Her questions for me would be more, like, what brand were the ratty sneakers Zalenka left on the bed?' Huh? Are you with me?

"And I'm like, 'Okay, they were New Balance.' See what I mean? Have I laid it out clearly enough for you?" He was blinking harder now; truth be told, he was pretty frightened.

But Mrs. Feeley was smiling again. Then she was setting the iron down. "Mr. Moon, you've been very helpful."

"I have?"
"More than you know."
"If you'll follow me in now, I'll take you to Henry the K."

5. MAJOR HELP
FROM HENRY THE K

Without another word, Mrs. Feeley led him through a fringed curtain and into a second room. A moment later they were standing before a gleaming brass elevator. Moon watched his guide's hand reach out to a row of illuminated buttons.

Soon they were gliding soundlessly along the elevator shaft. Moon was doing his best to hide his own hands, which were shaking noticeably. Would Dr. K be in one of his foul moods and chew him out viciously, as had happened so often before? How angry was he that People hadn't run the ass-kisser profile of him yet?

But now the mahogany-paneled elevator was easing to a stop. The doors hissed open... and they found themselves standing before a row of electronic scanners—dark glass eyes that flickered with occasional tongues of yellow lightning. A uniformed attendant in a gleaming, black-visored cap stood at attention nearby.

"Please step up to the scanners, one by one, and look into their eyes. Mrs. Feeley, you may step on through."

"Thank you," she said.

Moon stepped up to the scanners, one by one. Each one took a picture of his eye—a quick stab of bluish light—and

then the uniformed man waved him through: "You're good to
go, sir."

A few seconds later, they were walking down a long,
brightly illuminated hallway. At the end of it stood a pair of
massive steel doors that carried an enormous emblem of a human eye. Beneath the eye a black-printed legend read:

HENRY THE K

"Go ahead, push on through," said Mrs. Feeley. "Don't be
afraid."

Moon pushed.

And there he was—the smartest human being in the
world—sitting behind an enormous executive desk that glowed
bright yellow. For a moment, as his eyes struggled to adjust to
the brilliance, the stringer labored to understand.

Then he grasped it: the enormous executive desk was made
entirely of gleaming gold bullion.

It took Moon several seconds to find his voice, which
shook badly when he did. "Hello again, Dr. K."

The man behind the $150-million desk glared coldly at
him. "Hello, Moon. *Wie gehts*, eh? *Jawohl*! Uh-huh. You bet!"

"How are you, Dr. K?"

"*Sehr gut*. Terrific, huh?"

"Dr. K, before we get started, I want to apologize. I know I
promised you that we'd publish that glowing profile of you
soon: *The Eminence Grise: Still Playing at the Top of His
Game!*"

Dr. K nodded slightly, but his grizzled visage betrayed no
expression. "Fugg-ED it, Moon. Huh? Not to worry! EFF-re-
body writes me up as *The Eminence Grise*, top of his game.
Not zuch a big deal, eh? Anyvay, vat ist you want? Is dis de
bizness mit Harry Zalenka?"

"Yessir. They put me on it—I'm stringing for *People*. I'm
chasing the story. All kinds of problems. I was working with
Liddy for a while, but then he turned on me."

"Liddy? Hah!" One of the two famous eyebrows rose
slightly. "A fuggin' amateur!"

"Sir, he threatened to kill me with a No. 2 Pencil!"

But Henry waved this away: "Big deal, Moon, big deal. You know Liddy—he threatens to kill eff-ry one mit his pencil! Hah!"

Moon nodded. "Thank you, sir. Anyway... I came to you because I've been trying to figure out the Zalenka case, and it's too much for me. I'm not smart enough, sir! But you are... you're the only eminence grise on the planet who can unravel this one, Herr Doktor!"

The famed analyst of international *realpolitik* produced a thin, frigid smile. "One thing I can tell you now, right a-vay: Get off dat case, Moon!"

Moon stared at him. "That's funny. Liddy told me the same thing. He said the Zalenka story has 'Terminate With Extreme Prejudice' written all over it."

Dr. K nodded. "Lissen to me, Moon. Dere are tings mit dat Zalenka situation—you don't know vat you're fuggin with. Trust me on dis. You get too close, you maybe burn your fingers bigtime, know vat I mean? Hah-hah!"

"Yes, sir. I hear you. But unfortunately, I've already gotten into it. I'm neck-deep in it, sir. I don't want to waste your time, but there's one extremely intriguing aspect of the story I thought you might help me with. A literary aspect, if you will?"

"A literary aspeck? Vat are you talking about, literary?"

"Sir... as I'm sure you know, Zalenka was living in a motel room at the end, over on Maryland's Eastern Shore. A place called *The Evening Breeze*. Anyway, I managed to gain access. And I came upon a word—he'd scribbled a word on the countertop—a name. Samsa. Gregor Samsa, the tormented salesman in Kafka's story, *The Metamorphosis*. Do you know that story?"

Henry's famous face darkened noticeably. "Don't insult me, Moon! Of course I know dis story! Samsa is der salesman, selling der fabric all across der Germany, der Czechoslovakia, wherever. Huh? Huh? Ja! And he turns into der huge bug. Eh? *Jawohl!* Big bug, big bug! So vat iss your kuh-VEST-ion?"

"Very simple, Dr. K. As everyone in the world has known for fifty years, you are a genius at making connections. Well... do you see any connections here? Why would Zalenka write that name in his kitchen? Melvin Fishpaw told me he loved literature. He was a compulsive reader, apparently. He loved surreal fiction, loved the Theater of the Absurd. The Jabberwocky!"

Dr. K's eyebrow had risen again, was waggling again. "Jawohl. Go forward, putz! Jabberwocky vill not help us here! Vat is your kuh-VEST-ion?"

"Okay," said Moon. "So we know Harry was knowledgeable about Kafka. We know he understood the story. The roach crawls around on the floor of his bedroom for hours, while his family begs him to get out of bed and go to work. He's supporting them all, you know?"

"*Ja. Zehr gut.* Go forward!"

"Okay, but he can't leave the bedroom because he's a giant cockroach. He's stuck in there, eating lettuce and carrots and so forth. But then he makes a mistake; he opens the door a little, and his mother gets a glimpse of him."

"Yess, I remember ziss. Ziss is grotesque, but alzo comical, eh? And zee chief clerk, visiting the family, he zays: 'Something fell in there.' Ziss makes me laugh, ho-ho! Somethink fell in there, and he doesn't know it vas der cockroach what is falling off zee bed! Hah!"

Moon was listening hard, and scribbling notes: *grotesque, but comical. Something fell.* "Dr. K, please, sir. I'm asking you to dig deep here. You ran the Vietnam War for The Trick, for God's sake! You understand subtlety and ambiguity and deviousness better than anyone else in the Western World. When it comes to subtlety and ambiguity and deviousness, the rest of us are just lightweights, compared to you. So I'm asking you now, loud and clear: why does a washed-up alcoholic politico scribble the name SAMSA on the countertop of his fleabag motel? What was there about that story that so intrigued Zalenka? Were the bad guys knocking on his door at the moment he scribbled those five letters? Was the name supposed to be a clue that would tell a confederate what was taking place? Sir, is there a code of some sort, buried deep within the language of that immortal short story?"

Dr. K said nothing for a minute or so. Then, in a low voice, almost a whisper: "You are zinking too much, Moon."

"Sir?"

"I said, you zink too much here. You dodo! Zimplify, zim-plify! Ask yourself: Vat if diss is no literary code at all—vat if diss is simply a road map?"

"Sir?" Moon was gaping openly now. "A road map, you say?"

Dr. K was chuckling softly; he was obviously enjoying himself. "Tell me, Moon: Do you remember Villiam Carlos Villiams, the American poet—do you remember him zaying dat one time, zehr important: 'No ideas but in things?'"

Moon felt the hair beginning to rise along the back of his neck. "Things, sir? What do you mean, things?"

"I mean, not zee ideas in de book, not zee images in zee book, not the phil-ee-ZOPH-ee-cal concepts in zee book—but *zee book itself!* Zee book as object, Moon, zee book as *thing!* Maybe diz Harry Z hide somethink in zee book itself!"

Moon meditated. Cogitated. Ruminated. And then slowly, slowly, the light began to dawn. *The key to finding the tape… it's in the fucking book! Literally. It's in the volume of short stories,* The Metamorphosis. *Zalenka must have hidden the instructions—maybe a map?—maybe an actual key?—some-where inside an anthology of Kafka stories. But where? Where?*

There had been no books in the motel room; Moon was sure of that. Where would Zalenka have kept the book with the key to the puzzle in it? Where would he have hidden it?

Where was Zalenka living before The Evening Breeze? *Of course! His mother's place in Baltimore! Doris. Doris Zalenka. That night at* Almost Family!—*the interview he'd done with her…*

And then, all at once, he remembered the old lady's all-important quote: *"He's been living in my basement the last few years—with all his furniture and all his books!"*

A moment later he was shaking the great international thinker's hand. "Thank you, Dr. K. I can't thank you enough!"

Henry's right eyebrow cocked sideways a notch. "Zank you for vhat? I haff not told you anyzing! I merely spek-u-late—dat's all I do!"

"Oh yes, you have, sir. You've given me something huge. You've given me the key to the puzzle! Thank you. Goodbye, and a thousand blessings upon you!"

Less than a minute later, he was exiting *Whiz Cleaners* and running for the car.

6. THE KEY TO THE PUZZLE

Finding Harry Zalenka's bookcase was as simple as looking in the Baltimore *White Pages* for "Doris Zalenka."

The listing was actually for "D. Zalenka," but no matter. Harry's boyhood home—and his last residence before *The Evening Breeze*, apparently—had been located at 1214 Tower Oaks Avenue in the Roland Park section of the city, only three miles from downtown.

It was a tall, weathered Victorian pile with two gables and a mansard roof hanging out over the uncut lawn. By the time Moon pulled up in front, darkness had fallen over the graceful old Baltimore neighborhood. After parking the Sprint a quarter of a mile down the avenue, he hurried back to the Zalenka manse and spent a quarter of an hour casing the joint. And the fates were with him tonight; in less than five minutes, he was able to jimmy open a basement window and gain entrance to what he hoped would be the secret hiding place of the video-tape.

It took him another two or three minutes to creep sound-lessly along the three floors of the old house... until at last he stood motionless before a ceiling-to-floor bookcase in the moldering basement. *Moby-Dick, Life on the Mississippi, The Marble Faun, The Red Badge of Courage, The Great Gatsby*: they were all classics. But they were all by Americans—and not what he needed now. He took a step backwards, while his straining eyes continued to scan the cluttered basement. Frowning intently, he studied a glass-doored cabinet full of childhood games: Monopoly, Clue, Mr. Potato Head. Beside the cabinet loomed a half-size bookcase full of Proust and Flaubert and Dickens and Thomas Mann—the Europeans. He ran his gaze over the Germans until he found the small leather-bound volume he'd come here for: *The Metamorphosis and Other Stories*, by Franz Kafka.

The book fell open of its own accord to page 118, and he quickly saw why: a small beige envelope had been taped at mid-page, right below the title. He pulled the tape gently away from the page—he had a horror of marring Kafka's text—and as it came clear he read the opening line of the author's most famous story: *Gregor Samsa awoke from troubled sleep to find that he had been transformed during the night into a gigantic cockroach.*

He wasn't surprised when he tore the envelope open and found the small silver key waiting inside. Smaller than his little finger, the tiny key featured a racing Greyhound and a legend that had been pressed right into the metal: Wash DC *Downtown Greyhound Terminal, #141.*

Long he stood, pondering the silver key. Henry the K had been right all along: *No ideas but in things!* But the beige envelope also contained a sheet of folded typing paper. Squinting in the dim light falling through a nearby window, he scanned the note that Harry had left behind:

The key to the puzzle is the puzzle.

'Twas brillig, and the slithy toves did gyre and gymble through the wabe!

Bulletin: Our reality changed forever on a sunny November afternoon in Dallas, at the moment when the radio announcer barked into his microphone: "Something is wrong here; something is dreadfully wrong!"

Make no mistake: that event was the first step in the transformation of American reality. With that event, we entered the Kingdom of the Mirrors.

Hear me: on that heart-stopping afternoon, television was transformed from an entertainment medium into an environment. The infinitely powerful mirrors were erected and the theft of our vision began in earnest.

Hear me: the key to the puzzle can be found in Kafka's mighty line: "Gregor Samsa awoke from troubled sleep to find that he had been transformed during the night into a giant cockroach."

What is Samsa's dilemma, exactly? Simply this: his vision has been stolen from him. Blinded by mirrors, he is no longer fully human. Gregor Samsa has become a quintessentially modern figure: the human insect.

He stood there, motionless and marveling, for another minute. Brain whirling, he asked himself again and again what he should do next? Was he the only person in the world who knew where the Zalenka tape now lay hidden? Or were there others in the know... others who were perhaps already en route to the Greyhound Station on downtown "I" Street?

He started to dial Yang on the cell, then changed his mind. After slipping the key into the pocket of his jeans, he headed back toward the cellar window. But as he was climbing through the opening, he changed his mind again and hurried back into the dim basement to retrieve the book and return it carefully to its place among the Europeans. Then, moving swiftly, he hustled back down the circular driveway toward the waiting Sprint. Ten minutes later, he was back on I-95 and racing toward the nation's capital.

All right, he told himself, you gotta remain calm. They're watching you, and they're listening to you, but they can't read your mind. They don't know you have the key. You have to believe that. They don't have the technology for that. Not yet. They can't look in your pocket, because they don't have the technology yet.

Or did they? And if they could look in his pocket... couldn't they also read his thoughts?

He was about to find out. If they were picking up his brain waves, they'd surely be waiting for him in the Greyhound station. By now his hands were shaking so hard it was difficult to handle the wheel, but he hung on as best he could. The drive seemed to last forever, but at last he reached the Capital Beltway, exited at Georgia Avenue and then zoomed south toward downtown.

After another eternity, he found "I" Street and spent another ten minutes trying to park the car. But at last he spotted an open meter and got the little Chevy into the adjoining space. Then he walked toward the station, two blocks distant. He was tempted to run, but he fought the temptation and managed to control his steps.

Once inside, he strolled past "Locker Rentals, $3 Per Day," and was relieved to find the clerk dozing behind his plastic counter. The locker room was located beside a shabby-looking lunchroom, The Snack Shack, where two teenagers were flipping coins. The rest of the long, narrow tables were empty. Moon walked past the doorway of The Snack Shack and the teens looked up. "What's jiving?" said one. Moon said, "Not much happening, dudes." They seemed content with that, and resumed their coin-flipping. Moon strolled into the locker room—pale green linoleum and a hand-lettered sign in black Magic Marker: *Wash your hands after using these facilities.*

The key went into the lock without difficulty, and a moment later he was tearing the seal on a heavy brown shipping envelope. It contained a single videotape cassette. Just a black rectangle of plastic, with no distinguishing marks at all. It was Zalenka's mole-tape, and the entire Western World was looking for it.

Exiting the locker room, he closed his eyes and took a deep breath. If they were going to hit him, it would surely be now. But nothing seemed out of the ordinary—the teens were still flipping away, and the waiting room was still full of bored, yawning passengers. Would they nail him back at the car? No, the Sprint still sat where he'd parked it, gleaming fitfully in the streetlight. He could hardly believe his good luck. He had the tape in his hand, and the spooks were nowhere in sight!

What now?

He knew what. And he knew where.

It was time to pay a visit to BAR... time to spend an hour with the sculptor Ferg, and with Ferg's VCR!

7. YEVCHENKO AND THE CONGRESSMAN: VIDEO DRAMA IN ONE ACT

FADE IN:

BEFORE THE MAIN TITLES

INT. A DESERTED COCKTAIL LOUNGE—LATE AT NIGHT

Two men sit at a table in the back of the deserted lounge. They're both bleary-eyed, wiped out after a night of drinking.

Superimposed on this image:
Trader Vic's Lounge, Washington, D.C. February 11, 1980

Voiceover: This recording was made by accident, after the video camera was inadvertently left running by someone who'd left the lounge a few minutes before the images you are about to see were made.

YEVCHENKO

I hab some-pin for you, Gomery.

CONGRESSMAN MONTGOMERY
That's good, Yevchenko—because I have some-thing for you.

YEVCHENKO
What you got?

CONGRESSMAN MONTGOMERY
Big Bird is going up. It will be deployed before the end of the year. Here's a copy of the Secret Executive Order.

(He hands a document to YEVCHENKO)

This is fresh, Yev. This is current. This hasn't even gone to the Joint Chiefs yet.

YEVCHENKO
Dat is good. Dat is very good. Here for you, dis.

(He slides a stack of $1,000 bills across the table.)

CONGRESSMAN MONTGOMERY
Excellent, excellent, my fine Russian friend.

YEVCHENKO
(Lifts his glass)

We toast, my friend! Wod-ka, forever! Eh? Wod-ka!

CONGRESSMAN MONTGOMERY
Wod-ka, forever!

(He picks up the money, stuffs it in his
suit-coat pocket)

But before we part, I gotta ask you a question.

YEVCHENKO
Okay. Okay. What you Amerikanskis always
say? Shoot! Fire away!

CONGRESSMAN MONTGOMERY
Who did Kennedy, Yev? Who did JFK? I mean,
really. I'm just curious. Was it your team?

YEVCHENKO
My team? KGB? No, of course not. No KGB!
Kennedy and Oswald… dat was YOUR team!

FADE OUT

FRIDAY

1. "GET OUT OF THERE, MOON! RUN!"

After reviewing the contents of the Zalenka tape with Ferg and his Irish booze-hounds at BAR, Moon returned home, hid the videotape, fed Fang, and toppled into bed.

But his sleep was destined to be cut short.

At four minutes past seven in the morning, Yang was on the horn... and once again screaming at him. ". . . reporting deadline this afternoon, five o'clock, we got zero in the can, what the fuck —"

"Stop!" shouted Moon. "Stop now! I have news, Yang, major news!"

It took her seven or eight seconds to bring the screaming to a halt. When the air was finally clear, Moon said: "I got it."

"You got what, Captain Dip?"

"I got the tape, Yang."

"You're kidding."

"I'm not. Yang, I've got it. He'd hidden the goddam thing at the bus station."

"Bus station? Where? How?" A pause. Was she impressed? Or simply thinking about her next move? "You aren't telling me anything, Agent Smart."

"I sure am, Merciless Lady. I'm telling you *bingo*, Yang. I'm telling you *Eureka!* This is it—the 100-Percent Dead-Solid-Perfect All-Beef Enchilada."

"The Zalenka videotape?"

"Ten-four, commander."

"Moon, are you telling me that you've actually located Zalenka's video?"

"I am. I did. That's an affirmative your way, you Chinese ballcutter. We are good to go on the tape. He'd stashed it at the local Greyhound Station, right in the heart of Washington By-God D.C. I can hardly believe it. Holy cat shit, Yang!"

"Calm down, flotsam. You haven't told me diddly shit yet. What's on the tape, that's what I want to know."

"Oh... how about everything?"

"*Everything?* What the fuck does that mean?"

"Just what you'd expect it to mean. The entire ball of wax. The CIA mole and a Slavic gentleman named Yevchenko, toasting each other with wod-ka. Oh, and there's also a major money exchange. Lots of thousand-dollar bills going across the table, from Russia with love."

"I can't believe it."

"I couldn't either, not at first, anyway. We're going to win the Pulitzer, Yang. You and me—famous at last. Think of it!"

"Let me be sure I have this right, Moon. You're saying you have the CIA mole on a videotape being paid off by Gregor Yevchenko?"

"Correct-o. And then-Rep. Montgomery also distinguishes himself on the tape by presenting the Russkie with a Secret Executive Order authorizing the launch of Big Bird. The info was so fresh that the Joint Chiefs hadn't even been told yet."

"Astonishing," said Yang. "Inconceivable."

"Utterly off the charts," said Moon.

"So where are you?"

"I'm sitting in my apartment, where else? I'm staring into the very green eyes of a very hungry Maine Coon."

"What are you going to do next?"

"I'm going to try not to crap myself."

"Get out of there, Moon."

"My sentiments, exactly."

"Get out of Baltimore, and I mean now. You're carrying political dynamite on that tape, and some very powerful people will stop at nothing to take it from you."

Moon barked raggedly—a laugh? "My thoughts exactly," he shrieked into the Nokia. "You're reading my mind."

"Get moving," said Yang. "Get out of that apartment, you bozo. And don't go anywhere near your car. It's probably wired with 400 pounds of plastic explosive by now. Just walk away and catch a cab. Take it to Baltimore Penn Station and grab the nearest Metroliner for New York City."

"Ten-four, captain. I'm on my way."

2. ATTACKED BY A
NO. 2 PENCIL!

But when Moon tried to open the door of the Dump so he could run for a cab, he found that it wouldn't budge. Something was in the way... two somethings, in fact. They were legs, and the man to whom they belonged was a very familiar figure, indeed. Moon followed the legs upward until they dovetailed and became the midriff of a stylishly clad gentleman in an expensive, silken suit. This gentleman wore a pale blue handkerchief in his coat pocket and a very impressive-looking mustache. He did not seem happy to be greeting the stringer.

"Hello, Moon."

"Hello, G.," said Moon.

"You'll come with me now," said Liddy. "We're going to take a ride in your funny little car. Flight is useless, and you might not live through the attempt."

"Flight?" said Moon. "That never crossed my mind, Gordon. I was simply headed out to the 7-Eleven, hoping to purchase a cup of morning java."

"Right," said Liddy. "Walk with me, you sad little turd. I warned you to stay clear of all this foolishness, and you wouldn't listen, and now it's too late."

Having pushed the door open by now, he took Moon's col-
lar. "We'll walk to the car together. You'll climb behind the
wheel and I'll get in on the passenger side. I hope you won't
try anything stupid. Do you understand that you're in the cross
hairs, even as we speak?"

"Cross hairs?" said Moon. They had reached the sidewalk,
and the stringer was squinting through the early-morning haze,
looking for the sniper.

"Correct. You've been there for the past five days, virtually
non-stop. A lot of people are locked onto you, Moon, and
they're all prepared to take you down at a moment's notice,
should the situation require it."

"The situation?"

Liddy ignored this question, however. Moving swiftly, he
flowed around the front of the Sprint and quickly opened the
door on the passenger side. "Drive, my unfortunate friend."

"Drive?" said Moon.

"Let's take a drive through Druid Hill Park," said Liddy.
"And while we're driving, you can perhaps tell me where
you've hidden the videotape. We saw you glom onto it at the
Greyhound Station, so don't waste my time with your silly
denials."

"Videotape?" said Moon. Moving slowly and carefully, he
was easing the car out of its parking space and onto St. Paul
Street. The pre-rush hour traffic was still light. "What kind of
tape are we talking about, Gordon?"

"Oh, please," said Liddy. "This is so childish. We're talking
about the videotape that Harry Zalenka stashed in the bus
locker. The video he made of Senator Montgomery entertain-
ing Gregor Yevchenko at Trader Vic's. The same video he was
using to blackmail the senator, right before he disappeared. I'll
bet it's hidden right here inside this piece of shit you're driving. Really, you could save us both a lot of trouble by simply
digging it out and presenting it to me."

Moon nodded. "Okay, I know when I'm beaten, Gordon.
I'll get it for you as soon as we reach the park. But I hope you
don't mind if I ask you a question."

"What do I care now? You're history, caballero."

"Who is George Yarnell, aka Spider, and why did he send me to Fishpaw?"

Liddy chuckled. He had begun to stroke his silken mustache. "Yarnell works for the Company, excrement-for-brains. His real name isn't important. His job is to protect Senator Montgomery—and that's an *important* job. Why? Because the senator and a couple of his Democratic colleagues on the Intelligence Committee basically control the Company's yearly operating budget. We're talking billions of dollars here, you pathetic loser.

"The man you call 'Spider' knew the media would be swarming around The Evening Breeze after Zalenka's body was discovered... so he made sure he got there first. He went there under an assumed identity, and he was looking for the kind of journalistic chump who could be manipulated easily.

"That's you. Got it? He sent you to Fishpaw because that rotund shyster knew more about Zalenka than any other human on the planet."

Moon nodded. "All right," he said, "but I still don't get it. Why didn't the Agency simply kidnap Fishpaw and torture him until he revealed the location of the tape?"

Liddy smiled and stroked. "You're a bright boy," he said slowly, "but not quite bright enough. Don't you know there's a war on?"

Moon turned to look at him. "A war? Between who?"

Liddy released an unhappy sigh. "Between the dark-siders at the Company and the gumshoes at the FBI, of course. Really, Moon, were you born yesterday? They watch each other around the clock... which means they have to live by certain rules of engagement. And those rules are ironclad: If the Company nabs Fishpaw and sweats him, then the Bureau will instantly use its political and media contacts to expose half a dozen different scandals in the secret files that J. Edgar built.

"So their hands are tied, you see? Under the rules, they aren't allowed to actually hurt Fishpaw—all they can do is watch him surreptitiously and hope to pick up a piece of information that might lead them to the tape. Your tape, I mean. Do you see where we're headed here?"

"I think I do," said Moon. "It's pretty complicated, isn't it?"

"Absolutely," said Liddy. "It's downright labyrinthine, you inept imbecile."

"So Spider sends me to Fishpaw... who's actually playing on the FBI team... and Fishpaw tries to steer me toward breaking the story that would destroy Montgomery?"

Liddy smiled. "You're starting to pick up on it, lost one. But remember—Fishpaw doesn't know where Zalenka hid the tape, because Harry didn't want him exposed to that kind of risk. He'd told Fishpaw everything except that one simple fact."

Moon swung the Chevy Sprint left onto Druid Hill Drive. "Sounds like you've got it all figured out, Gordon. So tell me: do you also know what happened to dear old Harry Zalenka during his sailing trip on the Chesapeake Bay?"

"I do. I do. But first, you need some background—starting with the fact that when Zalenka initially came to Congress, back in 1981, Montgomery had already been there for several terms as a Democratic Rep. At that point, Montgomery was already a high-ranking member of the House Intelligence Committee—which meant that he had a security clearance and access to all kinds of top-secret info. That, of course, was how he managed to get his hands on the engineering specs for Big Bird."

Liddy paused, then growled with sudden laughter. "It's amazing, isn't it, how destiny works? Somehow, purely by chance, Zalenka left his video camera running one night at a back table in a famous Washington watering hole. Then he staggered off for another drink and got caught up in a lengthy conversation at the bar. While he was gone, the still-live camera accidentally made a seven-minute tape of then-Representative Montgomery engaged in a secret confab with a well-known KGB agent. Apparently, the tape was deeply compromising—since it also contained some discussion of the JFK assassination and Lee Harvey Oswald's possible links to the KGB."

Frowning, Liddy shook his head at the strangeness of fate. "At first, Zalenka was stunned and terrified by what he discovered—soon after he returned to the back table and retrieved his camera. Scared shitless, the Z man hid the tape in his attic and tried to forget about it. But as the years passed, poor Harry began getting too drunk too often. Soon he was a raging alcoholic and desperate for cash. And that's when he made his fatal mistake. He started to believe he could actually get away with blackmailing Nolan Montgomery—who was by then the all-powerful Chairman of the Senate Intelligence Committee.

"Delusional? You bet. Montgomery and his people tolerated the threats for a little while... but when Zalenka began vowing to go public with the tape, they had to act. They picked him up at The Evening Breeze Motel where he was hiding—he'd moved out of his mother's house in Baltimore by then, in fear for his life—and hustled him down to his sailboat. Then they set out with him on his final voyage. One of the senator's aides took him out with a Glock, and they weighted the corpse and sank it.

"They hadn't counted on one possibility, however—the chance that the corpse would inflate with gases from decomposition and bob back to the surface, even with the weights on it. As soon as they got word that his body had been found, they rushed it to their own morgue at Langley and cremated it.

"But somebody in the State Police blabbed about the gunshot wound to the head, and somebody in the Coast Guard blabbed about what he'd seen when the sloop came ashore." Liddy sighed mournfully. "People are such blabbers, Tommy, don't you think?"

"I do," said Moon. They had entered the park now, and the Chevy was drifting alongside purling Druid Hill Creek. "Turn down there," said Liddy, pointing to a narrow side road that quickly disappeared into a nest of overhanging tree branches. "You know, it's a real shame you had to get involved in all this. I warned you again and again, but you just wouldn't listen. Pull over and park."

Moon did as instructed. Then he turned the engine off. The two of them sat quietly, watching the late summer breeze ripple through the green leaves. The scene was deserted. "Okay," said Liddy. "Before we get too philosophical here, how about handing over the tape?"

Moon reached beneath his seat. It was that easy. The video was still nested where he'd hidden it the night before, still wrapped in the innocuous-looking *Burger King* carryout paper bag he'd found for it. "Thank you very much," said Liddy as he reached for the bag. On the word much, however, Moon saw a flash of yellow... the color of the No. 2 pencil that was suddenly zooming toward his eye! But the stringer had been expecting this, and at the last instant he ducked away from the thrust. He heard a crunching sound, as the No. 2 splintered against the driver's side window. And then Moon was out of the car and running. He looked back for a moment, saw Liddy waving the useless pencil stub and screaming at him: "Don't kid yourself, pal—I've got another No. 2 right here in my pocket!"

Still clutching the tape, Moon ran. Liddy crawled from the Sprint, then stumbled and toppled forward onto the gravel road. Moon ran harder. It was only fifty yards back to the creek and the road that ran beside it, and when he reached that road, he got a huge break. A whistling teenager in a bright green pickup was roaring along the gravel road, and when Moon loomed suddenly in front of him, he stood on the brake. The pickup fishtailed drunkenly for thirty yards, then came to a stop. In a moment, the stringer was pulling the cab door open and howling at the startled kid inside: "I'm in trouble—get me out of here!"

The driver hesitated, then shrugged. "Okay, what the hell! Let's do it." He stomped on the accelerator and the truck lurched forward. The tires caught... and a moment later, they were gaining speed and headed toward the park exit and downtown Baltimore.   Looking back, Moon saw Liddy running frantically down the road, his burly figure growing smaller by the second.

"Listen," he told the kid in the pickup. "I gotta get this package to New York ASAP. I'll give you twenty bucks to run me over to Penn Station. There's a Metroliner leaving in fourteen minutes."

"You're on," said the kid. He seemed to be enjoying the adventure he'd stumbled into. "Many thanks," said Moon. "Believe me, you're saving my life."

3. WITH YANG AND TOLLIVER ONE-TWO-THREE

He caught the 8:05 Metroliner just before it pulled out, and by 11:00 a.m. he was boarding the glass elevator for the ride up to the 37th floor of the Time Warner Building.

Would he puke? Would he collapse in a nerveless heap? How long was it since he'd eaten a decent meal? Three days? Four days? His mind was racing, screaming like the metal wheels on a roller coaster going too fast for the turns. Hang on, he told himself, *you're almost there. Just get the evidence into Tolliver's hands and then you can rest.*

At last the lurching elevator car crawled to a stop. The doors hummed swiftly open, and all at once he was staring into the mask-like face of a young African woman with strikingly high cheekbones and glinting disk-earrings the size of pie plates. Pinned to the dashiki-fabric above her left breast, a copper-plated name tag announced that she was Ashanti, the Time Warner receptionist.

"Hello, Ashanti," said the stringer. "I'm Tommy Moon, from Baltimore?" Brain swirling, he gaped at her as if he'd just arrived from the dark side of Pluto.

Ashanti stared dolefully at him. Her eyes were liquid gold, and enormous, and they watched him carefully... as if he were some exotic life form that at any moment might suddenly turn dangerous. "Can I be of help, sir?"

Moon gazed in wonder at her Frisbee-like earrings, at the emerald trapezoids of glowing tribal paint that caged her almond-shaped eyes.

"Baltimore!" he barked. "*People* stringer!"

She jumped, put one hand up to the long red slash of her mouth. "I need Tolliver," said Moon. "No... scratch that. I need Yang. Do you know her?"

Her tribeswoman's eyes took light. "Yang Yang?"

"That's her. Yang Yang!" Moon was nodding ferociously now, close to tears. How long could he stay on his feet? "Do you know her?"

"But of course, of course I do! Yang Yang! *People*! We share sushi together on many lunch times, House of Flashing Bamboo Curtain! Last year, we studied Tae Kwon Do together!"

"Will you please call her, Ashanti? Tell her it's Moon. Tommy Moon. Tell her it's urgent. Tell her I have the item. The item is safe; I've brought it all the way from Baltimore."

"Safe item?"

"Safe!" blared Moon. "Hurry!"

Ashanti nodded. Then she hit a yellow button on her console. A few moments later, a pair of glass doors to Moon's left slammed violently open, as if propelled by some implacable force.

"Moon!"

"Yang!"

"You're here!"

"I am!"

"You've got it!"

"I do!"

"Safe and sound?"

"Absolutely pristine!"

Yang fixed him with her razor-thin gaze. "So you made it."

"I did," said Moon. He held up the *Burger King* carryout bag. "I brought the Cheese Whopper with me, too. Hah! Hah! You can start applauding anytime you want, Yang."

"Shut up," said Yang. "Stop clowning. This is some serious shit, Moon."

"I know," said Moon. "It's even dangerous! Liddy warned me not to look for the tape. He said it would mean Terminate With Extreme Prejudice—instant death for anyone who came into possession of it. But as you can see, I'm not dead. Not yet, anyway."

Yang snorted. "Terminate? That's a bit melodramatic, don't you think?"

"Well, I know Liddy can be a tad flamboyant at times," said Moon. "But hey, I do think he knows his shit. He came very close to killing me with a yellow pencil."

Yang was shaking her head. "You can skip the Hollywood stuff, Moon. Are you ready to meet Tolliver?"

"I am. The question is: Is Tolliver ready to make his acceptance speech?"

She was glaring at him. She was black eyed and oval-faced, and with pencil-thin eyebrows: her starkly Asian features might have been an illustration lifted from a plane geometry textbook. "Speech? Speech? What the fuck are you talking about, Moon?"

"His acceptance speech, Yang—you know, at the award-ceremony? After they give *People* the Pulitzer for investigative reporting?"

She sneered. Ignoring him, she hit a button on the black-plastic surface of Ashanti's telephone console. "Tolly, he's here."

A pause. Then: "The asshole from Baltimore?"

"The very one," she said into the console. "He's got the goods and he says he's hot to trot."

Another pause. "Bring him to me, Yang. Bring him to the Inner Sanctum."

Yang stood up. "Congrats, Mooner. He's going to debrief you in his private barroom. It's usually reserved for U.S. Presidents and movie stars."

Moon grinned. "I knew I could be somebody one day," he said, "if only I worked hard enough to make it happen."

She snorted again. "It's not you he cares about, you nitwit. It's the Cheese Whopper. Follow me."

They hurried down a long, narrow passageway past rows of cubicles where frowning magazine slaves hunched above their computer screens.

INSIDE TOM CRUISE'S BATTERED MARRIAGE!

BRAD PITT, WHO'S SORRY NOW?

So this was it—the heart of the Time Warner labyrinth. The flickering ganglia-snarl at the core of the *People* magazine empire. Beneath subtly recessed ceiling lights, the chilled and conditioned air lay motionless as gelid vanilla on the flickering screens. By now the two of them were exiting the long rows of cubicles and stepping into a small, beige-painted sanctuary which contained a single desk and a single cyber-screen. The screen glowed pale blue, and a Zen koan floated there:

> *The one who knows he does not know:*
> *this is the one who knows.*

Yang led the way from the outer office through a small inset-door marked *Big Dog*. On the other side, a tall thin man sat on a curving bank of gleaming patent leather. He did not rise to greet them. His smile was pale and wan, and his college-boy hair looked like a shock of wavy, golden-brown wheat. His teeth were huge and brilliantly white—Moon thought of piano keys. Those are Yale teeth, thought Moon.

"So… the wandering hero finally arrives. Hello, Tommy Moon."

"Hello to you, Mr. Tolliver," said Moon. He held out his right hand. Tolliver took it for a moment, hung from it like an exhausted fish hanging from a line.

"Yang tells me you've come up with a major discovery."

"I hope so," nodded Moon. He lifted the *Burger King* carryout bag and shook it. "Everything we wanted to know seems to be on this tape. Zalenka made this video fifteen years ago, by accident. While boozing with a few congressional pals at Trader Vic's in Washington, he shot some video as a prank. But he'd inhaled a great deal of vodka during the party... and it made him careless. He left the camera sitting on a table while he headed up to the bar to gab with a bunch of congressional staffers.

"The camera was still running. Seven minutes later, purely by chance, it made a video of Senator Montgomery—today the chair of the Senate Intelligence Committee—talking with a clandestine Russian friend named Gregor Yevchenko.

"Later, Zalenka returned to the table and retrieved his camera. When he played the tape back and saw what he had, he could hardly believe it. Fifteen years passed, and then one day Harry discovered he was short on cash. He'd become a desperate alcoholic by then. He was frantic for moola, and he decided to blackmail the senator to get some."

"Bad idea!" said Tolliver. "Bloody shame. What sort of hanky-panky are we talking about here? What'd he give the Russkies?"

"Big Bird," said Moon. "On the tape, you'll see Senator Montgomery hand the Russian spy a copy of a Secret Executive Order related to Big Bird. You'll also see major money change hands. Then Yevchenko explains the JFK assassination... and the two men toast each other with wod-ka. This is some very heavy shit, Mr. Tolliver."

Tolliver sighed and shook his head. "I must say I'm amazed. I'm positively flummoxed, Moon. And here I thought you were just a little pinhead living on a back street in Baltimore! But please tell me: are all of these events you describe clearly presented on your tape?"

"With crystal clarity," said Moon.

"Oh, dear," said Tolliver. Then he paused for a moment. He was thinking. "So I guess the deal was... the senator and his aides on the Intelligence Committee responded to the blackmail by putting Mr. Zalenka into the Chesapeake Bay with a stack of diving weights attached to his belt?"

Yang had one hand in the air. "They also provided him with a bullet in the head, Tolly. No extra charge."

"All right," said Tolliver. "So they shot him first. Then they put him in the Bay. Tried to make it look like a suicide. Am I on it?"

"You're dead-solid-perfect," said Yang. "Boy, you don't miss a beat, Tolly."

"Thank you," said the executive editor. "I do try. Yale and all that, you know? But there's something here I don't quite get, Moon."

"What's that, sir?"

"Just call me Tolly, please. What I don't understand… if this tape is so hot that it could bring down a government, how did a dumb-ass magazine stringer from Baltimore manage to get hold of it? Nothing personal… but I do understand that you were educated at a public university."

"Good question," said Moon. "The truth is, I got some key help at important moments. Evel Knievel was very helpful, for example. Donald Trump made important suggestions. And Henry the K proved absolutely invaluable."

Tolliver was staring at him. "You got help from Henry the K?"

"I did," said Moon. "He gave me an important part of the puzzle. He's the real hero of this story, Tolly. He's the one who told me to look in the Kafka book. Let your fingers do the walking, he said, and I did. But it's also true that I'm a fairly smart dude in my own right. I used my native intelligence—don't forget that part."

"I see." Now Tolliver made a globby, snuffling sound. Yale laughter? "Yang here tells me that you've had quite an adventure during the past couple of weeks, my Baltimore *amigo*."

"I sure have. You bet."

"So how'd you figure out where he'd hidden the tape? Why'd you decide to look in his momma's basement?"

"Well, I majored in English literature at the University of Maryland," said Moon. "It's not Yale, but it was a solid education and it sensitized me deeply to literature. So when I found this word scribbled on a countertop… it took me a while, and I needed a lot of help from Henry the K, but I eventually started thinking about the fact that SAMSA was the name of a character in a short story by Franz Kafka. You see, this guy wakes up one morning –"

"Please," said Tolly. "I'm Ivy League, and I know very well that you're referring to the guy who turns into a cockroach."

"You're all over it," said Moon.

"Sheer brilliance," said Yang.

"Okay," said Tolliver. He paused for another Ivy League yawn and then drawled at the two of them: "Looks to me like the proof will be in the pudding, as they say." He pointed at the wacky-looking *Burger King* on the side of the bag: "Why don't we play that thing and see what's what?"

Moon nodded and pulled the tape from the bag. "Over here," said Tolliver. He'd put a languorous right hand on a TV console built into the wall. A VCR player rested beneath it. Moon slid the tape into the slot, hit play, and they waited.

Nothing at first. Then a blizzard of light, a deluge of swirling, glowing confetti across the screen.

Then Montgomery and Yevchenko, talking Big Bird and trading Big Bucks.

Yang was lighting a Pall Mall. "Wow," she said. "Who'd have thought this little prickster could pull it off?"

"Open and shut," said Moon as the two men on the tape toasted each other with wod-ka. "Well, looks like you've got him," drawled Tolliver as the tape came to an end. "No wonder Liddy was so uptight. No wonder he wanted to shut you down." He had produced a glass ashtray from somewhere. "Yang, I've asked you not to smoke those goddam things in here."

"Sorry, Tolly. It's the stress," said Yang.

"Is this the only copy of the tape in existence?" The executive editor had turned to Moon now.

"That's right."

"No other copies anywhere?"

"Not a one."

"Okay," said Tolliver. "Nice work, Moon. You've earned high accolades—and I have some very good news for you, young man."

"Really?" said Moon. "That's great. Thank you for the compliment, too, but I'm 51 years old."

"Age is relative," said Tolliver. "It's all in the mind. And I do want to congratulate you, Correspondent Moon."

"Congratulate me? How so? Correspondent? What do you mean?"

"You've just been promoted," said Yang.

"I have?"

"You're a full-fledged Washington Correspondent for *People* Magazine," said Tolliver. "As of this moment. You're now on contract—as soon as you sign this document, I mean." He had retrieved a sheet of paper from somewhere inside the desk. "According to this brand-new contract, you're now a National Correspondent at $100K per annum. And here's another wrinkle you're sure to like: the contract is for five years."

"Really?" said Moon. "Damn."

"Hubba, hubba," said Yang. "The onetime jerk-off is now king of the hill." She was lighting another Pall Mall.

"That is very good news," said Moon. "You see, I've got major college expenses coming, directly up ahead. I've got a teenager in Baltimore, bless her."

"Fret no more," said Yang. "That paper Tolly just handed you is worth half a million clams."

Tolliver sighed and shook his head. "Clams? Jeez, Yang, that expression went out 40 years ago. You need a more up-to-date phrase book."

"These developments are quite pleasing," said Moon, "and I really want to thank you both. But what about the story?"

They stared at him. Their eyes were droopy; their faces seemed downcast, wounded-looking.

"The story?" said Tolliver.

"Right," said Moon. "The cover story: *Murdered Congressman Had Inside Knowledge of Major Washington Spy Scandal*."

Tolliver smiled, then ran a hand through the wavy wheat-shock that was his hair. "Well, now," he crooned at his stringer. "I'm sorry to say, that won't exactly be happening."

Moon stared at him. "Not happening? What do you mean?"

Tolliver had removed the tape from the machine. Still smiling, he held it out toward Yang. "Babe, I can't take any more of that goddam demon weed. Get out of here, please."

"Aye, aye, sir," said Yang. She took the tape from him.

"Wait a minute," said Moon. "Where are you going with that tape?"

"I congratulate you, Moon," said Yang. "To think that you're now a bona fide *People* Correspondent, and not just a bottom-of-the-turd-barrel ordinary stringer. Talk about upward mobility—only in America!"

"Wait a minute," said Moon. "Hang on here, for shit's sake. I really think you should give me back that –"

"Have they cut him his first giant paycheck yet?" said Yang. Then she stepped out the door. All at once, she was gone. With the tape.

"You can pick that check up in accounting, down on the fourteenth floor," said Tolliver. "They've got it ready for you. Your first yearly check, in advance—the $100K we're giving you immediately, now that you're a National Correspondent."

"Just a minute here," said Moon. "Are you telling me –"

Tolliver laughed. His shoulders hunched way up, and he made a series of rapid little barking sounds. His large white teeth— Yale teeth—shone like buffed ivory beneath the overhead lights of the Inner Sanctum.

"Come on, Tommy," he said. He was still smiling. "We can't possibly run that shit at *People*, and you know it. We couldn't run that kind of shit in a million years. Are you fucking crazy?"

"What?" said Moon. "What? The Zalenka story? You can't run it?"

"Of course not," said Tolliver. "That story would be a threat to our national security! I'm sure I don't have to tell you what's at stake. I mean, you're a grown-up, am I right?"

"You're kidding me."

"Not in the least, my dear Baltimore friend. A story like that would trigger an earthquake in Washington, and the reverberations would cause enormous damage to this great old country of ours, all around the world. I'm sure you don't want to be a party to anything like that.

"And besides, I happen to have attended Yale University with Nolan Montgomery. We sang the *Whiffenpoof* song together, and I have no intention of allowing him to be pilloried on Grub Street. So there."

"I can't believe this, Tolliver."

The exec editor smiled warmly, and the soft vanilla light played sweetly along the piano keys. "I think you need a holiday, Moon. I really do. Maybe a couple of weeks in Jamaica? A few afternoons in your own private cove, maybe with a New York model, savoring the various rum concoctions of the region? Because you're wound too tightly, old soul; you're wound far too tightly for your own good.

"You need to learn to compromise. Huh? Learn not to take yourself so seriously! Life can be good, don't you see? There can be rum in large crystal tumblers, with chunks of tropical fruit floating in the liquid. You'll see. Let the river come to you, Moon. Let it flow. For once in your sad, masochistic life, stop mucking everything up and enjoy the music. The Zalenka story is dead. Okay? Even as we speak, Yang is shredding the tape and then incinerating the slivers. The evidence is gone, and life resumes. You're a National Correspondent now, and you're making the top dollar."

He sighed vacantly, a weary executive editor, fatigued by the heavy responsibilities he bore. "You didn't really think I was going to let you destroy Nolan Montgomery, did you? Hey, man... we sang the *Whiffenpoof* song!"

Moon blinked slowly, calmly at him. "So you're saying... it's over? We're going to run nothing more than the cartoon-story about the tragic congressman who drowned and the grieving women he left behind? The usual dreck? The usual empty soulless nothing? We're sitting on the story of the century, and we're going to run the usual *nothing*?"

Tolliver sent up his best smile. "What is your problem, Moon? Don't you want to be a National Correspondent, instead of a peon stringer eating turkey turds all day?"

"No!"

"Don't you want to make $100K a year, instead of $19 an hour, like some hapless supermarket checkout clerk?"

"No!"

By now, Tolliver had removed a strange-looking tubular device from somewhere inside his shaggy "Y" vest. It was a tube made of clear, hard plastic and outfitted with a metal mouthpiece. Amazed, Moon watched him suck greedily at the contraption. He took three or four rasping breaths.

"It's my rescue inhaler," he said. "I've got major-league asthma, and you've just brought on an attack."

"Have I?" said Moon.

"Indeed, you have," said Tolliver. "You're really serious about wanting to run this story, aren't you?"

"I am."

"So you're not going to accept the deal?"

"I don't think so," said Moon.

"But why not? Give me one good reason."

"The story," said Moon. "We have to publish the story."

Tolliver took a long pull at the rescue inhaler. "Well, that's just plain deranged, Mooner.   Listen to me, you self-destructive fuck. There's no way on earth that story ever runs in *People*. Got it? You're pissing up the maypole, hombre, and you know it." He took another giant hit from the inhaler, a hit big enough to suck all the oxygen out of the room. "This is the history of your entire life, isn't it, Moon? You win something—you win *big*, for a change—and then you throw it all away. Am I correct? How many years did you spend in psychotherapy, loser? Let me guess. I'll say five years. Okay? You spent five years with some pipe-puffing Freudian guy, but it ended inconclusively. Am I right?"

"On target," said Moon. "How'd you figure that out?"

"It's all over your face," said Tolliver. "Your face is a billboard, Moon, and the message is spelled out there for all the world to see. It's a one-word message with only five letters: L-O-S-E-R. Tell me again: where was it you went to college?"

Moon frowned. "The University of Maryland."

"See there? Tell me: Did you even try to get into Yale?"

"Nope."

"See there? You fucked up your college career, and now you're going to fuck this up, too. Listen to me, Moon: If you want, you can walk out that door right now, with all the problems of your life completely solved. Plenty of dough… a job with a high-prestige publication and a fat expense account. Success! For shit's sake, you'd be somebody, numb nuts!"

He took a giant rescue-hit: Swwwoooosssh!

"Well," said Moon. "I do think we have an obligation to our readers."

Tolliver stared at him. "You're kidding. Are you telling me you still believe that silly shit from Journalism 101? Get real!"

"They deserve our best effort," said Moon. "They're shelling out $2.79 for the book, and they deserve the best we can give them."

"Oh my God," said Tolliver. Swwwoooosssh!

"If there's deviltry loose in the heart of our Republic, they should be told."

"You absolute bozerino!" Swwwoooosssh!

"I don't deny that we're basically a Hollywood celebrity rag meant for lonely housewives," said Moon. "And I suppose there's a place for us in their silly cosmos. As a matter of fact, I'm only moderately ashamed of the fact that I work for you, Tolliver."

"I appreciate your kindness."

"But the fact remains: we're being tested here, and I'll never sleep soundly again if we fail to pass that test."

Tolliver's mouth hung open. It was clear that his day had been ruined. Swwwoooosssh! "Okay, then. Fine. So be it. But please let me be clear with you, Mr. Moon. Let me explain to you what will happen. May I explain?"

"I think I already know, but go ahead."

"Okay," said Tolliver. "First, let me remind you of the fact that you no longer have a Zalenka videotape. Yang has seen to that. Second, both Yang and I are fully prepared to refute anything you ever write or say about these matters. Third: There will always be two of us, and only one of you.

"In legal parlance, you're fucked. No editor or publisher with even a shred of survival instinct will ever disseminate your silly little tale of kidnapping and federal government hanky-panky. Are you getting the picture? Is all becoming starkly clear?"

"Crystalline," said Moon.

"There's more," said Tolliver. "Once we pass the word about your attempt to harm national security with your irresponsible journalism, you will lose favor with your Dear Old

Uncle Sam. You will probably face a scrupulous IRS audit or two in the years directly up ahead. Your whole life will be scrutinized carefully in the search for past lapses that might somehow still be prosecuted. Shit, you could even have a fatal highway accident... or suffer a drug overdose that will be seen as a direct result of your raffish, rebellious lifestyle. Do you see where I'm headed here?"

"I do," said Moon. "I see it, and I'm properly frightened."

Tolliver pointed the rescue inhaler at the stringer. "Good. I'm glad to hear it. Now what are you going to do?"

Moon thought about the question for a few moments. He frowned. He shook his head. Then he sighed and consulted his watch. It said: 11:59

"The thing is," said Moon, "I've already gone and done it."

Tolliver glared at him. "Done what?"

"Do you know the Latin verb *publicare*?"

"What? *Publicare*? What the fuck are you talking about?"

"I've already *publicare*-d, Tolliver." Moon turned, pointed at the big TV screen affixed to the back wall of the Inner Sanctum. "Do you get cable?"

"Cable TV? Of course I do."

"Can you bring up CNN?"

Tolliver gaped. "Can I bring it up? You silly fuck... we own CNN."

"Bring it up. It's noon... time for the latest headline news on CNN!"

Tolliver's right hand had gone to his shaggy "Y" vest again. Now it held a mini-remote, which he aimed at the blank screen. They waited while the device blossomed into light.

Wolf Blitzer was yakking away at his breathless best. ". . . has scheduled a press conference in the Capitol Rotunda for 4 p.m. That's four hours from now, and CNN will take you there live. Meanwhile, we're going to be covering these shocking developments in detail for you throughout the afternoon.

"To repeat: the chairman of the U.S. Senate Intelligence Committee, Virginia Senator Nolan Montgomery, has resigned his senate seat amid startling disclosures, confirmed by the FBI, that he sold spy satellite secrets to the former Soviet Union in the early 1980s."

"Holy rat shit," said Tolliver. "No! Oh my god, we are so fucked." Swwwoooosssh!

"Smile, Tolliver," said Moon. "You and your Yale buddy are about to become famous."

"But how did you... how did you break this goddam thing? You told me and Yang that was the only copy of the tape!"

Moon smiled happily. "There's a little barroom in the heart of Crabtown," he said quietly, "and the name of that barroom is BAR. And the bartender there is a crazy sculptor guy named Ferg."

"Crabtown?"

"Baltimore. Dear old dirty Baltimore. And Ferg has a younger brother, Little Billy, who works for the Bureau. He's a G-Man, and he's my friend."

"I see. So you made a copy of the tape and you passed it on to the Bureau, via this... this *Billy*—because you knew they'd do everything they could to give the Company spooks a black eye?"

Moon grinned at him. "Not bad, Tolly. You know what?"

"What?" The editor was glaring fiercely at him now.

"For a guy who went to Yale, you're actually pretty bright! And here's the good news for you and Yang: I'm not going to tell anyone how you tried to kill the story of Montgomery's treachery... or how you tried to bribe me to join you in the cover-up. I'm not going to say a single word, ever."

Swooooooosh! The dazed Yale alum was shaking now, shaking as if palsied. "You aren't going to say anything? Thank you! Thank you! But why?" His eyes narrowed. "What do you want in return, Moon?"

"Nothing," said Moon. He gave the exec editor his best smile. "I don't want a thing from you, Tolly." But then he paused and frowned. "No, wait. There *is* one thing. I want to keep my current job."

Tolliver stared at him.

"What? What? I can't believe it. After everything that's happened, you still want to be a *People* stringer?"

"I do. I do. It's the only thing I know how to do. And anyway, I've still got some unfinished business to take care of."

Tolliver blinked at him. "Unfinished business?"

"That's right," said Moon. "The Sinatra interview. I still haven't gotten that Sinatra interview!"

4. THERE'S NO PLACE LIKE HOME

The two of them were sitting together at the 29th Street *Burger King*. It was 24 hours since the sudden resignation of Senator Nolan Montgomery—and the shocking new disclosures about the drowning death of Harry Zalenka—had appeared on newspaper front pages and network news shows all around the world.

"You did a great job, Dad."

He smiled at her. "Thank you, Keera."

"You turned out to be a mighty fine reporter... even if you are only a stringer!"

"Again I thank you, honey bun." He was watching how the overhead fluorescents winked and gleamed against the metal in her orthodontic braces. He liked that. He liked it a lot.

"I love you, Keera. You're mine!"

She leaned across the plastic table and squeezed his left shoulder with both hands. "I love you, too, Dad."

He picked up his soft drink. "Life is good, sweetie pie. You'll be going into the tenth grade in a couple of weeks, and you're gonna be a knockout!"

"Oh, Dad," she said.

"I mean it," he said. "An absolute knockout."

They sat quietly for a bit. It was twilight, and they sat at their table near the back of the 29th Street eatery, smiling and sipping their Cokes while the streetlights flickered on outside the eatery.

"This is fun," said the stringer. "I'm where I want to be, Keera."

She peered at him earnestly. "And where's that, Dad?"

"With you," he said.

5. HURT ALL OVER AGAIN
BY MR. SINATRA

Frank Sinatra made a pistol of his right hand.

He aimed it at the stringer's nose.

"Not you again!" he barked. "Who the hell are you?"

"Me? No problem! I'm a stringer, sir. For *People.* You know, the magazine?"

The famous blue eyes grew much larger. Frankie was obviously pissed. "How the hell did you get past Arnoldo and Rocky? This is the third time you've crashed my dressing room in the past six months! Why won't you take no for an answer, you little moron?"

"Could I interview you, sir? I'll keep it short, I promise. Three minutes would be terrific. Two minutes, even. Perhaps we could get it all done in 45 seconds—I think that would work, if you're willing to give it a shot! Here you are, sir, 79 years old, at an age when most performers.... "

Sinatra began to scream. They were the screams of a world-class baritone, so they came across loud and clear. "Hey! Hey! Arnoldo! Rocky! Who is this guy? Who *is* this guy? Who is this guy?

"Who *is* this guy?"

THE END?

The increasingly befuddled but laughter-loving author of *The Stringer* resides in Hastings, Michigan. You can reach him at tomnugent@sbcglobal.net, should you have a question that isn't answered for you in this volume.